D1230592
Stand Alone Novel

Plague in the Mirror

PLAGUE IN THE MIRROR

DEBORAH NOYES

CANDLEWICK PRESS

This is a work of fiction. Names, characters, places,
and incidents are either products of the author's imagination
or, if real, are used fictitiously.

First edition 2013

Library of Congress Catalog Card Number 2012947257
ISBN 978-0-7636-5980-6

13 14 15 16 17 18 BVG 10 9 8 7 6 5 4 3 2 1

Printed in Berryville, VA, U.S.A.

This book was typeset in Rialto DF Piccolo.

Candlewick Press
99 Dover Street
Somerville, Massachusetts 02144

visit us at www.candlewick.com

For Jill

People like us, who believe in physics, know that the distinction between past, present, and future is only a stubbornly persistent illusion.

—Albert Einstein

A Disturbance

There's a certain kind of silence when you wake in the deep of night, in a strange bed, knowing that someone has entered the room.

You don't know how you know. Your eyes are closed, and whoever it is hasn't made a sound.

But the silence is thicker than usual; it weighs more, in the way that a withholding friend is worse than one who's just neglecting you.

With that weight, that knowing, on her chest, May opens her eyes to find a figure at the foot of the canopy bed.

At first, she can't make out more than a luminous outline, but as her eyes adjust in the dark, she sees it's a girl, looking as surprised as May feels.

The intruder's hands hang at her sides, and the folds of an old-fashioned gown puddle on the Tuscan tile at her feet. May has the urge to clap her hands over her eyes the way you do when you're a kid and think blindness and invisibility are the same thing.

You can't see me.

Me.

Because as the other girl walks forward in the moonlight, it's like looking in a mirror. The ghostly stranger might be her identical twin or a fainter version of May, who can't look away or cry out or move.

The girl extends both arms and tilts her head. Her fingers open and close like anemones, and May helplessly watches her run a palm over the satin bedspread, fingertips disappearing into the fabric. Lifting the cloth of her gown to kneel, she works her way up the length of the bed with hands on either side of May's rigid body, a mean, knowing smile blooming on her face. She sits down, weightless, right on May's midsection. "*Ciao, bella.*"

May tries to squirm free—"Get *off!*"—but there's nothing to repel. The girl is both there and not there, and it's paralyzing.

"So, you will speak to me in *inglese? Come mia madre?*" As if to answer her own question, she slides a short, savage-looking knife from the folds of her dress and holds it by May's clenched jaw, the milky-pale blade never touching skin. "No? I would show you what Cristofana thinks of *no*"—the knife disappears again—"but I cannot." Her voice dips as with a secret, an expansive gesture taking in what might be the room or the whole world. "I knew I would find you. But not where or when."

May lets out her breath to object, but her voice is useless, gone.

"Oh, stop trembling, *sciocca*. I won't harm you." The ghost girl sighs theatrically. "Not today." She rolls away, an acrobat springing to her feet.

May watches her—it—pass effortlessly through the closed door, dissolving into the wood. She curls toward the wall, feeling her limbs unlock, her breathing slow to normal. She waits for her voice, a sob or a gasp, an earsplitting scream, anything, but the middle-of-night silence wins out, and some sane part of May knows that's best. She instead conjures her mother's voice from childhood, that firm, low, loved voice, soothing *Shhh . . . it's just a dream*. The room is hushed, gentled, but only for a second, because this dream won't behave like one; it won't wear like dreams do.

Just breathe.

Fixing her gaze on the digital clock face, May watches an hour pass, and another. She tracks shadows on the ceiling, naming the shapes they make—*tree, wolf, teeth*—and every time she shuts her eyes, the scene loops through her brain again: a bleached, weightless figure crawling beastlike up the bed and over her; the transparent glow of the knife; but most remarkable of all, the face, her own exactly, and as alien as the moon.

So May keeps her eyes open.

An Old, Dark Heart

Stifling her yawns over continental breakfast, May comes to as Gwen folds her newspaper closed. Their summer rental in City Center East opens today, and May knows that Gwen will hustle them out of the temporary B&B to beat the heat and the lunch crowds.

"Dude," May says, leaning too conspicuously toward Liam, "walk me to my room so I can pack."

He moves to stand, no questions asked, but his mother halts him with a hand on his arm.

Gwen's used to them, but it's been almost a year since Liam and May have really hung out—that is, before he shuttled over on the Volainbus Monday to fetch her at the airport—and now May isn't a part of anything bigger anymore. She's just May, alone in Florence with friends of what-used-to-be the family, and her summer guardian is overcompensating.

"You're not packed yet?" Gwen asks.

May decides to just come out with it. "My room's haunted." Her voice is kidding—the morning light has calmed her, settled over the terror of night like a layer of snow—but she still feels it, the heat of fear. "I think."

Li gives her that measured, bemused look May somehow forgot until this moment, the brotherly I'm-waiting-for-you-to-start-making-sense look. Li isn't her brother. Technically, he isn't family at all. Neither is Gwen, who went out of her way to help Mom and the teachers structure this as an independent study to sub in for May's final exams. But May's known these two all her life, and in a way, they're better than family. Especially now.

"I guess I had a nightmare," she admits, half believing it. "And I didn't want to hang around in there and pack alone."

Gwen's smile is tight with concern. "It's normal, you know, with stress. Bad dreams . . . insomnia . . ."

Oh, please. Don't start. May covers her ears, humming like an angry hive, and Gwen regards her watch with a shrug. "All right. I'm here if you need me. I'll line up a cab. You two need to get cracking."

There's no trace in the room to suggest that the girl was there.

"Sleepwalking?" Li theorizes from the rumpled bed while May sits on her backpack to crush down its contents.

He looks like a deposed prince in jeans and Converse lying with crossed ankles under the antique canopy, at home as can be on a sea of silk covers. May hides her smile. She must have looked wrong in that bed all week, too, an imposter. The B&B villa is in the hills that circle the city, on the site of what used to be a vineyard, according to its brochure, and before that a medieval nunnery. Li and Gwen arrived exactly a week earlier than May did and hadn't yet exerted themselves in her absence. They mostly enjoyed the villa's blue, blue pool, the grassy hedges and banks of red flowers, or walked north in search of wine and olive-oil tastings in country farmhouse shops. The first thing Li did when May arrived was plunk down her bags poolside, and show off the pink tan line under his collar.

"Maybe you woke up," he adds now, "or half did, and saw yourself in the mirror." They both look over at the tarnished glass above the dresser, its dark frame carved with sinuous lilies. Their reflections stare back, expectant. "That would've scared the crap out of me."

May struggles with the zipper on her pack and nods; as a kid, she was known to sleepwalk. "Yeah. That makes sense." She feels stupid, pitiful—the way he's looking at her—because if it was a dream she can't seem to wake up from it.

On the other hand, May thinks, with a glance at her childhood best friend, she doesn't feel invisible anymore, the way she did watching her mother deflate at the airport checkpoint when she thought May was out of range . . . or at the gate, locked in a half lotus on the hard airport chair, flip-flops askew on the carpet, iPod cranked to vibrate, trying not to meet anyone's eyes because her own were wet. No matter how loud May had thumbed the volume, she still felt mute and vanished, locked in a struggle not to let her mother's tired face, the obvious relief to be sending May away, be her last memory of her family. That invisible feeling was hard to shake even once she touched down in big, busy Florence. But Gwen's kept them so occupied this week with walking tours that May's had little time to feel sorry for herself, and they haven't seen City Center yet, so today will be even busier.

On her knees, May works the zipper closed and rests her head on the overstuffed pack, yawning. She swivels and rolls flat on the floor, the intricate mosaic tiles cooling her back.

"You didn't sleep," Li acknowledges, "did you?"

May covers her eyes with a forearm. "Guilty."

He heaves himself off the bed and lifts her backpack, gently prodding her with his foot. As he slings the pack onto his shoulder, May props herself up on an elbow. In the silence, she's tempted to tell Li what really happened last night, or what she thinks happened, because unlike her parents or Gwen, he would at least *entertain* that something weird occurred (and May still can't convince herself it didn't). He'd joke it to death, sure, and rob it of every hint of strangeness and mystery; he'd make her feel silly, but he'd make her feel safe.

All her life she's felt safe—more or less sure of herself and her place in the world—and now the people who gave her that are back in Vermont, dismantling home, stripping certainty away.

The idea that May's freak twin might be more than a dream is a lot like the fact that her parents are splitting up and forcing her to choose between them. It fits no known pattern of security.

Li's still waiting with her heavy pack on and a hand gripping the handle of her suitcase, so she offers one of her own hands like a hook, and he hauls her up.

Gwen's rented a small, airy third-floor apartment in City Center East. They cab over and settle in, opening doors and drawers, calling dibs on rooms, napping awhile. Later they devour the biscotti and mandarin soda from their landlord's care basket, enjoying the river view from the terrace. The sunlight has turned everything gold, and the temperature has dipped to bearable, so Gwen leads them outdoors and north toward the historic heart of the city a half dozen crowded blocks away.

Crossing to Piazza della Signoria is like parting the Red Sea. There are people everywhere, streaming in the same direction or trying to chisel a path in the opposite one. The narrow, shaded streets echo with the bleating toy horns of Fiats and the wasping drone of mopeds.

As they enter the piazza, May sees dozens, possibly hundreds, of people milling around in bright summer outfits. They chatter and squint up at carvings tucked in niches, pursue restless children pursuing pigeons, back into one another while framing photographs, and line up at carts to buy trinkets and limonata. High above them all, the sun-gilded tower of Palazzo Vecchio casts its long, welcome shadow over parched piazza stones.

As soon as she spots it, Gwen makes a beeline for Michelangelo's *David*, lingering until Liam and May jar themselves out of whatever sensory stupor they're in and sidle up beside her. She explains at length that it's only a copy; the real statue was moved indoors to the Accademia long ago, and May dutifully takes in David's furrowed brow and blank eyes. But she can't help it; her gaze slips down the famous torso to the statue's nether regions. She clears her throat and turns to Li, who's pursing his lips with a considering nod. They shrug at exactly the same moment and steer Gwen away, marching her past the surging horses in the Fountain of Neptune in search of gelato.

The fountain's spray cools May's cheek as they pass, and she tries not to let the flags swaying high in a still-hot breeze or the writhing bodies and muscled lions and screaming women on tall marble pedestals in the loggia unnerve her. Instead, she focuses on the crop of art students sketching side by side on the stone base of a nearby building: heavy-lidded boys; fashionable girls; a middle-aged woman in a plaid beret. They seem so content there, alone but together.

May follows a few more blocks north, lingering on the street while Gwen and Liam duck into a narrow gelato shop. They find her sitting on unoccupied steps within view of the cathedral and hand hers over—chocolate, always—and after they all dig in, Gwen points out Giotto's campanile and Brunelleschi's dome, il Duomo, in the distance.

"The last time I was in Florence," she tells them, "a friend brought me to a department store somewhere near here. Rinascente, I think. There's a rooftop café there I'll take you to. Seeing all this from on high is amazing, but you know that already. I think we'll be right at home in the apartment, don't you? We lucked out with our views."

May and Liam nod vigorously but go right on excavating with their little shovel-shaped plastic spoons, eyes downcast, devoted. They'll develop a pretty successful work pattern in the days to come. The two of them will take in another mosaic or wax-work or painting of the Virgin and Child; Gwen will buy them ice cream.

"You learn so much about a place through its art," she's rhapsodizing between dainty bites of lavender-fig gelato as they stand as one and start to walk north again. Looking at May, she asks, "Did you know your mother was studying art history when we met at school?"

Mom likes to paint — every few years she drags out her easel and invests in fresh tubes of acrylic — but May had no idea she studied art formally. Her urbane mother would appreciate it here — all these frescoes and gap-eyed statues, all these people bustling around in nice shoes — way more than May does.

And suddenly she feels overwhelmed by it all, not least the exquisite bulk of the domed cathedral they're now approaching. With its dizzying stripes and bold arches, its geometric intricacy of white-and-pink-and-green marble, the structure Gwen identifies as the Basilica di Santa Maria del Fiore seems to take up several city blocks. They sit down on another set of stone steps to take in the view.

May has never seen anything like it.

The only stillness on these swarming streets, it seems, is the architecture: stone and stucco and salmon tiles, shuttered windows and ancient, crowding towers. Even the sun is moving, May knows, casting longer and longer shadows, marking time. She feels ashamed of her own indifference, of how little she deserves this.

When May doesn't comment, Gwen stands up with

a glance at Liam. "I'm off in search of a cup of coffee. Meet you back here in twenty?"

May nods up at her, heartsick somehow. The strangeness of her surroundings has taken hold, and with it a sadness she wasn't ready for. Because it's over now: the mindless quiet of a Vermont morning; waking to the smell of Dad's coffee and a fuzz of green in the window, to Mom's old radio playing softly in her home office, barely audible under the mounting chorus of the birds; all that ease and sweetness. "What are we doing here?" she asks aloud.

"Here on these steps?" asks Liam. "In Florence? On Earth? Can you be more specific?"

"Gwen never should have let you take that philosophy class," May complains, with a knuckle-punch to his forearm. She doesn't want to be lousy company. Not here. But before she can explain herself, the ghost girl from the B&B intrudes into her thoughts again.

"You know why we're here," Li says lazily. "To help Mom with her book."

May's gaze lights on a glowing figure in the shade at the edge of the cathedral, which turns out to be a little girl in a gauzy sundress, blowing bubbles with a wand. "Remind me?"

"Historical travel guide for eggheads . . . like the

one she did about London? You know, what composer's buried in what tomb in what cemetery, and where do all the bohemians drink their coffee, and where were all the queens beheaded. You get the idea."

Gwen teaches medieval literature to grad students and publishes seriously wonky papers in her area of expertise, May knows, but also moonlights as a popular travel writer.

"My tuition's coming due, so she signed on for two more guidebooks in that series. You heard it here: it's all tombs and dungeons from now on. . . . Evidently everyone thought this would really cheer you up." When she doesn't respond, he adds, "Did you think you were here to soak up the Tuscan sun and eat ice cream?"

May tries to play along, but it's more of an effort than usual. "And we're really too old for camp?"

"I've been thus informed."

"Why didn't you stay home and work?" she asks seriously. "You're moving out in the fall anyway."

"Mom's on sabbatical. You know what that means. She sublet the house. Home's on wheels with her, always has been." He meets her eyes intently for the first time all day. "Are you OK?"

She's never thought much about Liam's eyes, which would be like thinking about a zebra's stripes. It's inconvenient, in a way, to notice them now, but they're a shocking blue. She glares at him.

"OK. It's lame and sentimental," he says — circling back now, aware that he's pushed too hard — that May isn't ready to talk about her family or the lack. "I guess I came because this might be the last time I get to really hang with my mom . . . and now you . . . before college. Even if it means I have to spend all summer in cathedrals." They both look up at the vast structure in front of them. "You're getting a stipend, at least. I'm doing this for free."

"Sucker," she jokes, because that's what they do — joke, soothe, smooth it over, whatever *it* happens to be — but May is relieved when Gwen returns, jittery with excitement.

"I've found something." She waves them off the steps, her voice soft, urgent. "Come, come. Quickly."

Liam groans, heaving himself up and startling a pigeon pecking on the curb nearby.

Gwen's long gray-white hair swings with her purposeful stride, and they follow past the office of the Misericordia to a narrow alley leading away from Piazza del Duomo toward Via dei Calzaioli. The fleeting daylight barely touches it. "It's called Via della Morte." She stops short. "Way of Death." Gwen runs her finger over a plaque, paraphrasing in that clipped, breathless way that pays homage to their joint minuscule attention span. “Around 1343, Ginevra, a daughter of the noble house of Amieri, fell in love with a young man from an unsuitable family in an opposing order. Her father forbade their marriage and made her marry a man named Francesco Agolanti instead, who was of equal birth. During a rash of plague, she took sick and seemed dead, so her husband buried her in the family vault in that cemetery between the cathedral and the campanile. In the middle of the night, Ginevra came to in a panic, terrified. She managed to unwind her bandages, raise the stone slab, flee from the vault, and return to her husband’s home along this alleyway.”

Gwen regards them with wide eyes, turning to the plaque again. “When Ginevra knocked, Agolanti was understandably shocked and took her for a vagrant spirit, barring the way, so she hurried to her father’s house in the Mercato Vecchio, where she was also rejected. Finally she tried the home of her true love, young Rondinelli, and was received by his parents. Her marriage to Agolanti was annulled, and she was able to marry Rondinelli at last.”

This is the kind of morbid-romantic anecdote that excites Gwen beyond all reason. She already has her camera out and is trying to get an atmospheric shot of the alleyway before the light goes.

Unimpressed, May and Liam linger with their backs to stone.

"Yay for plague," Liam offers. "I love a happy ending."

"True," Gwen agrees absently, framing another shot. "It's a bit like *Romeo and Juliet*—only with a better outcome."

Intervention is the trick with her, so after conferring behind her back, May and Liam wait for Gwen to let the camera rest on its strap around her neck; then they link arms with her, steering her gently out of the alley and into the waning sunlight of the piazza.

"You guys really cramp my style sometimes," she complains, laughing. "Listen. You haven't exactly worked hard yet, but why don't you take tomorrow off? We'll give each other a break. But only if you track down those photo permissions I asked for. This week. And, May, I'll need at least an outline for one of the three papers you're writing this summer. Also this week. Time management, dearest."

May nods.

"What'll you be up to?" Liam asks as they walk. It's sweet, in a way, how he's so protective of his mom. May supposes he's always been that way, at least since his dad left. It's just more noticeable here.

"I have an appointment at U-Florence. An old friend was on a team that recently exhumed a skeleton from a mass grave in Venice. They're claiming it's the first evidence of the vampires mentioned in contemporary documents.

"This is related to our friend Ginevra," Gwen continues, "in a way. The focus of the dig was mass graves of plague victims on Lazzaretto Nuovo Island. Around the time this woman died, in the Middle Ages, people believed plague was spread by what they called vampires. Not the bloodsucking kind. These spread disease by chewing their way out of their shrouds after they died, so grave diggers muzzled suspects with a sort of brick. The skeleton my friend found had a stone slab in its mouth."

"How'd they get the vampire idea?"

"I guess blood sometimes leaked from a corpse's mouth, causing the shroud to sink in and tear. U-Florence says this is the first forensic example of these so-called vampires. It's being contested, of course. Another archaeologist claims to have made a similar find in Poland."

"Battle of the archaeologists," quips Liam, rolling his eyes, and May tries to smile back.

Glancing vaguely down another twisting alleyway

of stone and shadows, she thinks how strange it is that such a sunny country, with more tourists and flavors of ice cream than seem possible in one universe, has such an old, dark heart.

Living Proof

At dinner it takes a while to find a *trattoria*, *osteria*, or *ristorante* — all basically the same thing, Gwen allows — serving anything remotely vegetarian. Tuscans love their meat, their tripe and wild boar and liver and sausage, and May has a feeling she's going to be eating a lot of white beans in tomato sauce for the next few months. *Thank God for olives*, she thinks, which is funny. As the child of confirmed agnostics, she isn't one to contemplate God, but in Florence, images of sinners and saints are everywhere, and heaven and hell look like very real places.

They focus intently on their food, not talking much over dinner. The outdoor tables were all taken when they arrived, but they scored a window seat and everyone seems lost in their own thoughts and flavors, content to half listen to the accordion-and-clarinet music out in the piazza or the warm murmur of Italian, English, German, and Japanese conversation at the tiny tables crowded into a dim dining room. But Liam finally speaks, suggesting they head up to Fiesole tomorrow, walk around the ruins that Gwen mentioned on the walk over. "I know it's only been a day, but I'm already up for some green. That B&B spoiled me."

May meets his eyes. "We're like some old married couple," she quips. "I was thinking that exact thing when we sat down to eat."

"As long as you start on the permissions, I don't mind where you go," says Gwen. The sun has almost set, and the square swarms with tourists in shorts and fanny packs. Gwen points out a little procession of formally dressed locals—Italians, anyway—meandering in their direction along the piazza's pedestrian zone. They approach in pairs or loose groups, the women impeccably made-up and holding their backs straight for smiling escorts. Not a few of the younger men strut solo in pointy shoes, but it's all moving at a snail's pace.

"Parade?" Li asks innocently enough, but an old man with chiseled cheeks, eavesdropping at the table behind them, tut-tuts.

"*È passeggiata, ragazzino.*" His tone is equal parts nostalgia and dramatic scolding (tourists!), and when he turns back to his companion, the men bend low and commence gossiping—at least it sounds like gossip—in energetic Italian that opposes the languid, almost choreographed stroll taking place on the pavement behind plate-glass windows.

May rests her napkin in her lap, sits back, and enjoys the show. It's a bit like running into a flock of rare birds out on a hike; you don't know what to call them, and you don't mind not knowing.

If there's one thing Italy has taught May so far, it's to value mystery.

She gets up before Liam does the next morning, and with Gwen already out and no one to muscle him out of bed, it could be hours, so May decides to take a slow stroll of her own. She scribbles a note urging him to swing by Pegna for picnic cheese and olives if she isn't back by the time he wakes up. Then she grabs the most compact guidebook in Gwen's pile—one with lots of pictures. For some reason, May has a burning desire to find some trinket for her mother.

Dad always says, "Thanks for thinking of me," and politely files away any remembrance she brought him. But Mom loves gifts, not expensive ones, just what she calls "mindful trifles." As a kid, May showered her mother with pictures, compositions of all kinds, handmade ornaments, feathers she found in the yard. Mom did the same, slipping cryptic notes into her school lunch, leaving a perfect round pebble in the dish where May kept her rings.

Mom and Dad have always been yin and yang, light and dark. Dad makes her laugh. Mom makes her think and feel—usually a frustrating kind of longing or impatience; Mom is so self-possessed, off somewhere else in her mind, even when out walking the dog. May isn't invited along anymore. Not since she was about eleven, when she took to rolling her eyes whenever her mother enlisted her. Secretly, May loved the walks, loved racing ahead up the path to the conservation land beyond their house with their border collie, True, crashing alongside through the brush, but some defiant part of her wanted to be asked twice, begged even, wanted to be indispensable, and her mother never begged.

Maybe May blames her mother for that, too.

In any case, Mom is going. Leaving them both, if that's what May decides—that her mother should move back to Boston, where May was born, alone.

It's up to her to choose by the end of the summer which parent she'll betray. Dad seems to expect it'll be him, but May isn't so sure. She only has one year of high school left. It doesn't make sense to blow it all up now. Couldn't her mother have waited one more year? Maybe it *doesn't* matter since in another year May will go to college, but the choice is there, meanwhile.

Don't make me choose. It was all she thought about, every time she looked at one of them, all through their tender, well-meaning lectures about why this thing was inevitable and how much they both loved her anyway and how she had nothing to do with any of it and they were sorry she would suffer in spite of that.

Still, May feels driven to find some small important object for her mother, who blames herself, May knows, though she won't admit it. Dad's more the grin-and-bear-it type. Maybe May blames her mother, too—for the divorce, for everything—and a gift, however thoughtful, won't conceal that fact. But still.

She knows Mercato Nuovo is somewhere south of Piazza della Repubblica, that it's nicknamed the Straw Market because people used to sell hats and baskets there. Now the stalls sell leather goods and souvenirs. Gwen said to get there early, before the other tourists wake up or the sellers shut down for the hot hours.

It isn't a long walk, but it's strange being out in the echoing streets by herself. The morning is overcast but warm and muggy, and she wipes sweat from above her lip, catching sight of what looks like the market loggia and the small fountain housing a big bronze statue, *Il Porcellino*, that she remembers seeing in the guidebook. Children flip coins into the water, some climbing on and caressing the boar. She remembers reading that if you feed it a coin, landing it in the grille below its snout, you'll have good luck.

The air is slightly cooler by the fountain, and she sits enjoying its faint mist on her cheek and arm for a moment, dragging her hand across the murky, greenish surface. The market stands are beginning to open now, so she wanders north, nodding at the smiling vendors with handbags, colorful scarves, and jewelry to sell. Nothing seems a match for her mom, though May stops to admire beribboned boxes of marbled paper. It's beautiful stationery but not special enough, so she makes a mental note to come back if she can't find a more unique offering.

The city is really waking up now, with women in fashionable suits clacking past on heels and children clustering outside idling cars en route to school. She heads back toward Piazza della Repubblica, crossing under an arch and trying to avoid the crowds gathering outside sidewalk cafés where waiters in red jackets bustle back and forth.

Then, on instinct, she veers off course completely. She can always fish out her map and find her way back to the apartment later. She's always been like this — at least since her parents learned to let her be independent on trips — willing to be lost. It makes her late a lot and frustrates other people, but it's led to adventures over the years, like the time she wandered into a street cordoned off by a film crew in Montreal and got to watch them shooting a car chase. It's also led her into some bad neighborhoods.

She walks a long, long time until she's in view of one of the old medieval walls snaking and climbing along the city's edge. Unlike some cities she's visited, Florence never seems far from the wide open, and because it's a hilly street, she can see green in the distance.

May stops to rest on a stone bench near the entrance to a residential courtyard, her gaze shifting to the early-morning light cupped inside it, a buttery, soft light saturating the white sheets and women's silky slips hanging at haphazard angles on laundry lines. She sees glimpses of green in the courtyard, too, a massive climbing flower vine on a trellis, potted lemon trees, a jumble of terra-cotta flowerpots filled with plants. The golden light filters through their colors like a kaleidoscope, hypnotic.

And that's when May sees her. The girl from the dream.

She's standing among the rustling sheets, barely visible, a milky shadow of a girl identical to May, a girl who flickers and fades as she shifts position. May can't ignore her. They're looking right at each other.

The ghost girl stops just shy of the courtyard gate, out of view of others passing on the street. She waves May over.

May shakes her head, her heart loud in her ears.

The girl parks a phantom hand on a phantom hip. "Have you *no* curiosity?"

Home in Vermont, pinned on the corkboard over May's desk, is one of her favorite quotes—by Dorothy Parker—about how curiosity cures boredom but there's no cure for curiosity. Her parents fed her that line of thinking all her life, and old habits die hard, it seems, because May is curious, insanely curious, though she won't say so yet. Not to this girl or anyone. It's easier to stay under the radar, in Pityville, where no one expects much.

She hesitates.

"You do wonder, don't you? Where I come from? Why I look like this?"

This? May thinks. *Me. You look like me exactly. Only you're not real.*

The sun's movement is beginning to affect the light. May can almost see a bar of morning brightness trailing the tops of the shuttered stucco buildings around the courtyard. She manages to open her mouth, breathing out the word, a question. "Yes?"

The girl's laugh is less amused than pitying. She stares back as if weighing every last one of her private options; the delay is maddening, and finally May can't stand it anymore. There's a roiling in her head, like a storm building. "Well, where do you come from?"

"I won't tell you," she challenges. "I'll show you. You are ready?"

"Ready?" *Are you crazy?* May looks around . . . for a way out, a witness, a sane bystander. The street is strangely deserted.

"Come." The girl—May remembers her calling herself Cristofana—holds out a hand and drops it again.

"Will I look like you if I go?"

"You already look like me, *bella. Esattamente.*"

"I mean, will I be a ghost?" May can't believe she's even having this conversation.

"Will you know the difference?"

Staring back at the girl, she thinks, *How do you know?* It's infuriating but also flattering, in a way, since everyone else, even Liam, would rather pretend May is fully present — a former, better version of herself — and not, in fact, a hollow automaton going through the motions. Her tired mind is playing tricks on her. "Is it safe?" she asks. "It can't be safe."

"Do you always carry on so? *I* am proof of this. Living proof."

"If you call it living, Ghost Girl."

Cristofana steps closer, her phantom basket swaying. "Spoken like a true authority."

May won't get up and back away. Part of her, the curious, scientific part, would like to reach out and see what happens.

If someone asked her to describe the ghosting precisely, she'd tell them it's like looking at a black-and-white photographic negative. Before digital, Gwen used to keep a darkroom, and when Liam and May were old enough, she taught them how to develop the long reels of film and make prints. On her ghost twin, the areas of definition or shadow, what would be the blacks in a final print, are bleached; the highlights/whites and midtones/grays are transparent.

"Long ago," the haughty stranger says, "in the year of our Lord 1347, I caught a sparrow in my hands and sent it through my *portone*—you have this word? *Doorway*, I think—to test this magic. In the bird flew and out again two hours later, still with the same piece of straw in its beak."

Tell her no. "If I could actually see you, I'd call you nuts," May complains, resorting to sarcasm to mask her fear. *Just no*. "But you must have turned sideways or something and the not seeing you part has me doubting myself—"

"You are bitter company, *bella*, a great disappointment to me, but I have picked you and have no one else to share my story with."

"But *why* me?"

"Your soul remembers what you do not—and shone for me like a star in the dark of time. There is only one of it and two of us, but you live in this layer of time and I in another. A soul exists in many layers; the soul's container or likeness in only one."

"We share one . . . *soul*?" And now May identifies that unfamiliar stirring inside: foreboding, dread.

"It would very much amaze you, what can be accomplished with our wills."

Does May have a will? Real and unreal are seriously mixed up at the moment; they have been since she arrived in Florence, since home ceased to be a refuge and people started flinging untenable choices at her.

"I am a pale shadow of myself . . . without will or action or substance. I can affect nothing here."

May looks away, lowers her voice. "Can anyone else here see you?" She feels the dread coiling now, like a dragon, all through her body. *Don't give yourself away. Don't start shaking.*

"If they do, it is as you see me, as a ghost. They doubt their eyes and hurry past. I try not to be seen. It confuses them and draws attention. You I enjoy confusing."

"Clearly."

"And yet I like you."

"I can't say the feeling's mutual." But a smile twitches on May's lips. There's a rush in all this, a crazy rush. Like it or not, she's blundered into something extraordinary, impossible, and it's hers. It might be scary, but it belongs to her alone. "Weren't there other generations? You said something about 1347? If what you say is true, our . . . soul had other lifetimes, right? Maybe lots. Between mine—"

"Enough. Do you suppose you have earned my secrets? I assure you, you have not." The ghost girl's voice is clipped, but her smile's indulgent. "I found you. That is all. And I offer to show you my Florence in turn. Do you accept?"

With dread before and behind her, May floats a moment in the ensuing pause, outside herself. "All right. Yes."

"Then follow carefully."

May rises from the bench like a sleepwalker and crosses to the archway. She trails Cristofana into the rustle and hush of the courtyard, into a tunnel of swaying, pale laundry shot through with light, toward an empty stone corner at the courtyard's far edge— and then out again, with her head roaring.

May feels hollow and nauseous, held in check by gravity only. Cristofana, on the other hand, is solid, all color and hard line. She's delighted with her trick. She applauds it, right there in what appears to be an alleyway behind an abandoned shop.

Luckily, this street at the edge of the city is even more deserted in Cristofana's world than it was in May's. As her twin marks a course, a sideways 8 on the stone near where the portal must stand—the sign for infinity?—May juts out first one arm and then the other, and her arms are a luminous outline. She looks just as Cristofana did on the other side . . . *a pale shadow of myself . . . without will or action or substance.*

But there's no time for astonishment.

Cristofana's off like a shot, navigating winding

streets and alleyways at the edge of the old city, moving with a stealth and grace that seem remarkable now that she's flesh and bone.

May floats after, faint and amazed, through the gate and along the river.

As they traverse the city's undeveloped edge, Cristofana points out the rolling green hills beyond, where sheep graze and men stoop in fields, where distant, soldierly rows of olive groves cast stark shadows and larks swoop overhead. There's not an airplane in sight. It's profoundly quiet, even this close to the center of the city. The sky's a rich blue laced with cottony clouds. May's afraid to touch anything—afraid of what *without will* really means—but she can't get over how beautiful Old Florence is, an alien, slimmed-down version of the city she's only just getting to know back with Gwen and Liam. For the moment, she's happy observing.

Without a word, they work their way back along angular, cobbled streets full of strutting roosters and rooting pigs, and soon there are people everywhere, though no buzzing mopeds or bleating horns, no blinking streetlights or shining glass.

May can't help glancing down at her arms from time to time, pivoting them in front of her, milky-transparent in the shade but mostly not visible at all.

She seems to fade completely in direct sunlight. When she finally finds the nerve to run her hand along a wall, her fingers pass effortlessly through stone and brick. She still feels hollow and sick to her stomach, a little headachy, but also light and free, more like water than flesh. Emboldened, she tries walking through a closed door. It works, and she turns on her heels in what looks like an empty peasant's hovel lined with straw, and she walks out again, giddy with success.

Smiling at these antics, Cristofana cautions, "Stay in the sunlight. Remember, it confuses others to see you . . . what there is to see." She squints at May as if taking mental measurements. "They think they see a ghost."

They come out into the open sunlight of a different piazza—long, rectangular, columned—surrounded by looming stone towers, some almost eighty feet high and shadowing wooden stalls, pavilions, carts, benches, merchant stands. The place looks like some kind of medieval movie set, full of men in red and blue and brown capes, women with wares laid out on their blankets, and girls with raw pink hands offering baskets of dewy pears and plums.

"Here is our market," Cristofana says, her voice patiently instructive, like that of a teacher introducing a new student to the class, and then—abruptly, as she seems to do everything—she darts down a long, narrow side alley, hooks a few lefts, a few rights, and marches them right back to the site corresponding with the courtyard in Florence Present where a faint, chalky sideways 8 marks the base of the portal.

"Oh," May says, blinking, almost disappointed. On the other hand, the queasiness and headache are starting to wear on her.

Cristofana stands very still a moment, lost in thought, the gaping, invisible doorway somewhere beyond her, May presumes. When they first approached from what she now realizes was the future, May's *present*, the portal had felt more like an absence than a presence, a blank summoning.

"You remember," Cristofana begins, again patiently, like an adult speaking to a panicked child, "I told you I flew a bird through this doorway, and out it flew again? I have also flown one bird out and, following after, captured another, like the first in aspect, to fly back the opposite way. The first, from my world, did not return. It remained in your Florence . . . many hundreds of years away. . . ."

May can only shake her head. No.

"The second, from your world, built a nest in a tree outside my window, fully fleshed, feathered, and beaked. It was an even trade, you see. My studies cherish balance."

"What are you trying to say?"

"I beg your indulgence just once more. This time, *bella*, I will go through alone and take the *portone* with me, so that you do not blunder in after and lose us both in the wilds of time. Stay nearby. Let the market amuse you until I return." She points. "It is that way."

"Are you *out of your mind*? You're not seriously going to *leave* me here? In the freaking Middle Ages?"

"I won't be a moment." Again . . . that patient smile. "Forget yourself, *bella*, your pettiness and fear. Look around, and be humbled. There is a first for everything, for all great leaps of knowledge, and you are making history."

Before May can cry out or leap forward, her double steps through the *portale*, reeling what looks like a mirror-sheet of fabric in behind her, erasing herself in a hot streak of black light.

At the same moment, May feels jolted, shocked by what can only be the return of her real form. What was a whisper becomes a roar. Sounds are amplified, distant cart wheels and hammering. Smells rush in—manure, river mud, cat piss, lavender. Her headache is instantly gone, along with the queasiness. Her blood feels like it's humming in her veins, and for a moment, May turns and turns, trying to take in her own form, veering into walls, disoriented and jumpy. Things calm down, but it takes her body a moment to adjust to "normal," return to itself. (*Unite with its soul?* she wonders, incredulous. *Their* soul, hers and Cristofana's. The same soul—now here and there at once.)

The panic is swift and intense as it dawns on May that she's flesh, visible, vulnerable. Feeling trapped in the alley, she stumbles over loose cobbles or a curb, toppling forward, falling hard. The pain is searing and she knows there's a cut on her leg, a big one, but she rights herself quickly, bolting onto a dirt cart road crowded with rooting pigs.

You can do this, she tells herself. *It's just like being out on your own, in the present, except your guidebook's no good.*

Some things are the same, some few architectural landmarks—Florence is an old city—and she knows that the cathedral will still be there, though maybe not all of it and with a simpler facade, and May thinks she knows how to get back to the market. She sets out confidently in what feels like the right direction, nodding at those who pass, avoiding their curious looks and whispering.

As the frozen moments pass, she feels less scared or stunned and more sick and pissed that she had the bad sense to trust Cristofana, an obvious liar and lunatic, just because she happens to have a trustworthy face. But then May realizes that people are actually crowding in on her, pointing and jeering. They've never seen anything like her. An old woman crosses herself. A young man in formfitting—that is, bulging—tights and a short, stained tunic steps way too close, leering into her face. He has winey breath, and his bad teeth are bared, his head tilted like a curious dog's.

At last, when something hard and slimy—a rind of chewed orange, May thinks—hits the side of her face, she panics and bolts, takes off running with the murmuring crowd collecting behind her. Darting down a narrow side street, she zigzags onto another tight block enclosed by sinister towers. Everything seems to press in and loom over, so she makes for the light between buildings, runs down one claustrophobic street and the next until she can see sky, plenty of it, and keeps running until there are few and then fewer and then no people in view.

She locates what must be a wealthy neighborhood—well-spaced residences with courtyards and small gardens or rows of potted fig trees between—darts out back and steals a plain-looking blue dress from a laundry line. Checking that her phone's still in the rear pocket of her cutoffs—for all the good it will do her now—she slips the dress on over her tank with shaking hands, almost laughing out loud. Who'll believe this? Gwen will sign her into the nearest mental institution when May tells her.

Tells her *what*? How do you explain what even you don't believe?

Something tells her not to abandon her own clothing, so May wads it into what appears to be a moth-eaten baby's blanket and slings the bundle over a shoulder. The only problem now is shoes. She has nothing to replace her patterned flip-flops, but the dress is long enough to drag along the ground, so it might not matter. She rehearses holding the fabric forward with her free hand to conceal her feet.

Returning as purposefully as possible out to the street again, May spots a group of boys advancing from the direction of the medieval gate and the green hills beyond the city. They're rough and rowdy, herding a sheep between them, so she turns back toward the city center, trying not to conspicuously hurry, but they keep pace, the poor sheep bleating in complaint.

Feeling less exposed but still edgy, May at last ducks into what looks like a public shop, its door propped wide open, though she can't read the painted script on the sign dangling from chains over the entryway. Inside, chickens bob around and three young men are seated at easels of varying sizes. The two nearest the door watch disdainfully as she limps in.

But when the third, the man near the far wall, looks up from his easel, squinting in shadows, he seems to look *into* her — or that's how it feels — and it knocks the wind out of her chest. He's crazy beautiful, for one thing: a long, tapered face with a dimpled chin, the classic Roman nose, an expression that makes her cheeks burn. Below thick brows, his amber eyes are a liquid darkness, like coffee.

"Sì?" he asks politely, apparently on behalf of everyone, though the other two only squint warily back at him.

"*Mi dispiace*," May tries, speaking directly to the man but dropping her gaze. Even when she can't see him anymore, May feels him watching her, and when she finally summons the nerve to meet his eyes again, they seem lit from within. He looks genuinely curious, intrigued even, and she's so grateful for this kindness that she wants to hug him.

"Forgive me," May tries in English, in case "I'm sorry" isn't archaic enough, lowering her voice because in a weird way it's just the two of them now. He probably doesn't understand her English *or* her Italian. What year is this? It's a little late in the game to be asking the question now, and to be honest, May doesn't care anymore. She can't believe this is happening. She can't believe, looking again into those eyes, that it's never happened before.

The man shrugs. No, he doesn't understand her any better than she does him. He looks poised at the edge of his seat, and his eyes roam over her as if to solve a puzzle or answer some penetrating question. But the search stops somewhere in the neighborhood of her knees, and his face clouds with concern.

One of the other artists has already turned back to his work with a baffled shrug, but the second, wiping plump hands on his tunic front, continues to monitor the exchange, watching with somewhat stern interest as the man at the back of the room stands up.

He's young, with a tangle of dark hair and skin the shade of caramel, so tall he seems to stoop just slightly to put the world at ease. But there's nothing slumpy about him. He's lean and muscular, rangy like a wolf, and though he hesitates for what seems forever, all May can think, stupidly, watching him cross to her, is *Oh, my God.*

He kneels at her feet, his long hair falling forward, concealing his eyes. His hands have the same rough beauty as his eyes and close urgently around her calf, giving her what amounts to an electric shock even with the bloodied fabric of the dress between them.

"*Stai sanguinando*," he tells her, glancing up, but May can only tilt her head like a confused animal, because she has no idea what he's saying, no real thought in her head at all except that his voice is deep and a little hoarse and so compelling that he could be reading her death sentence and she wouldn't stop him, and her heart is still thumping hard from what happened outside.

He leads her back to his shadowed workstation. His puzzled eyes linger on the flip-flops a moment, darting to and from her eyes as he raises the hem of her dress discreetly, working at what must be more than a scrape (it's finally dawned on May that her right shin is wet with blood, enough to soak through her stolen dress), sopping the wound below her knee with the hem of his linen shirt, his full mouth pursed in concentration, and she's all but shaking with shock.

He is touching me, she thinks, almost hysterically because she can't calm down, can't manage to take all this in. *A man is touching my leg in medieval Florence. The most beautiful man in the world is touching me, and he is a man*, she thinks, *not a boy*.

He can't be much older than May, but he has what she can only imagine is a man's smell, rich and strong and spiced with the secrets of his trade, walnut oil and shaved wood and turpentine. He moves like a man, capable and sure, his white shirt stained now with her blood.

As he rises and crosses to the big fireplace, where he sets about clanging iron pots and rooting around in the lengthening shadows in search of something, he leaves her skin burning with absence. May feels greedy to have his hands — scarred and paint-and-blood-streaked but beautifully brown and strong-veined and sure of themselves — back on her, and when he returns to lead her to a chair by the wall, urging her to sit, she feels her whole body sigh with relief.

He kneels again at an angle, lifts her leg apologetically, and props it over the hard plane of his thigh. His hands go to work again, cleaning the wound with a wet scrap of linen torn from his shirt, lightly smoothing away pebbles embedded in her raw skin with his thumb. Every stroke is electric, despite the pain beneath it, and May suddenly remembers a morning last summer, alone on a dock in Maine. The sun was just rising, and there was a steady breeze, more than a breeze — a teasing wind — blowing over the surface that made the skin of the water shiver in dancing, swooping spirals, made it rise and shimmer and fall and rise, and that's how her skin feels now, wherever he touches her, restless and shining.

By the time her medic concludes, pressing her hand

over the cloth he's tied to the wound, applying an instant's extra pressure, May's whole body feels quavery and strange. With him at their center, her surroundings have locked into focus. Everything is clear and vivid, alive in her senses as if the room itself is breathing, as if together they have become the room's heartbeat.

But in her peripheral vision May spots the pudgy painter peering from behind his easel, his eyes full of judgments she can't guess at, and the spell is broken, her moment's calm absconded.

What's more, there's a clamor out on the street, one that quickly draws the two disapproving artists outside.

If not for his mysterious patient, the man at her feet would go investigate, too — she can see he wants to; he's torn — and when May gestures that he should go, he nods, quickly covering her hand with his to assure she's applying enough pressure to the cut, sending another charge through her. He touches her cheekbone lightly, a feather brush with his knuckle. His knowing smile warms her through, and then, as quickly as the artist entered her life, he leaves it.

May sits very still a moment, following him with her eyes, watching him disappear, impossibly confused. She's almost relieved to find her reflection looking back at her then through the shop's display window, though there is no window, of course. No glass, anyway, just shutters opening onto the street. On the other side, Cristofana in ghost form smiles gravely and hooks a finger, beckoning.

Somehow May had forgotten.

How long has she been back?

May suddenly feels exposed, unsafe, more vulnerable than ever. It must be the look in her double's eyes: smug and scheming, the look of a lion about to take down a wildebeest.

"Please," May says in a voice more confident than she feels, "are we done here?" Her right leg's really hurting now, but curiosity demands a detour, and she manages to limp calmly to the rear of the workshop and peek at the charcoal sketch on the beautiful artist's board: it is terrifying, a sort of female gargoyle, its powerful neck extending from the edifice of a building, craning out over a fiery city where hundreds of thousands of tiny figures huddle together, indistinguishable and doomed in the shadow.

It's incredible and terrifying, nothing like the flat, formal paintings in all the old churches May's been visiting, thanks to Gwen, or like the Madonna and Child riffs on the other two men's easels. The sketch is a nightmare as modern or at least as universal as anything May's ever seen, and the paradox makes her ache. She felt so safe with him in those few minutes — as safe and seen as she's felt for a long time — but who would keep him safe? Where did visions like this come from?

May limps obediently to the front of the room, because in the end, she has no other guide, no other way out. She follows the shadow of her double — who's also limping, May notices, also bloody at the knee (probably more so without a bandage), though the blood on her long gown, like the rest of her, appears opaque — back to the abandoned alley and the stone wall with its faint sideways 8.

May slips back into her own clothes, leaving the blue dress in a heap at her feet, and at Cristofana's nod steps through without a word, without looking back, onto a hidden archway on a modern street full of buzzing mopeds and schoolchildren in uniform, a street blessedly free of Cristofana.

Fearful Rumors

When May finally works her way through Liam's barrage of texts and finds him, in the shade of a stone loggia in an outdoor café near the apartment, drinking a limonata, she hugs him over the iron railing, hard.

Caught between sitting and standing, Li is pretty obviously mystified. When she pulls away, he straightens to his full height, letting his hands fall from her shoulders, but one floats up again automatically. Long fingers brush her cheek. "Are you *crying*? Shit, May.

What happened? Why didn't you answer? I texted you like a million times. . . ."

She casts a greedy eye over the street: parked cars, the still facade of Cinema Edison. "Let's go?"

He walks around the railing to her. "I thought I saw you go right past me in the piazza, but you were in a mad hurry—"

"You saw me? How did I look?"

"You looked—is this a trick question?—distracted. Busy." He eyes her up and down. "Anyway, you weren't dressed like you. I only thought it was, I guess. But I figured you'd text me when you were ready to go. . . ."

They're standing on the sidewalk, in the shade of an awning on the corner of Via degli Strozzi and Via Pellicceria, squared in by four hunkering churches. As they start walking down Pellicceria, past Banca Nazionale del Lavoro, May remembers with relief the odd little building with the bright-lilac roof that Gwen explained was a betting booth. Already men and women are milling around it, consulting their papers for upcoming dog and horse races. Next door is the post office, which she also remembers passing this morning, with the same old men out front all meticulously dressed in their suits and polyester vests, rattling their newspapers, arguing politics and racing odds. All familiar. Good.

She touches the nearest wall—smooth, real, *now*—tears streaking her face. "I'm losing it, Li. What time is it?"

He shrugs, glancing at her leg, his eyes wide with worry. "I dunno. Ten thirty, maybe. You're shaking." He lifts his fingers to wipe the damp from her face again, almost reflexively. "You're not losing it. You just got lost."

"You have no idea what an understatement that is." She feels too stupid to look at him, but he lifts her chin with his thumb.

"Hey, it happens. Didn't you bring a guidebook? You didn't, did you? I knew it. Did you even bring your phone? You weren't gone long, but you always text back, so I got . . . worried."

Ten thirty. She'd left the apartment just after nine. How could she have been through all that—Cristofana and the river and the man in the artist's workshop—in the time it took to get to and from Mercato Nuovo? Impossible.

It worries her, how calm she feels now that it's over, how accepting. Does madness come over you that quickly, like a wool blanket thrown over your head . . . and you just learn to live in the dark? This calm adaptability is almost worse than whatever's causing these weird delusions. She thinks of her guidebook and phone in her bag and smiles. She thinks of the man's amber eyes looking right into her, the feeling of his warm, capable hands on her skin.

"You hurt your leg. You OK?"

May nods. She is. Now. The bandage, though, is mysteriously gone, and a scab's already forming.

"Let's get out of here, huh? This city's like a maze. It's starting to get to me. And I'm tired of all these people."

She puts out her arm, and he links his through, looking away. When he doesn't ask it out loud—*what happened?*—May is glad. She can concentrate on breathing. On taking one step and another. Liam's so easy, so steady. Always has been.

They find the depot and don't say much, waiting to board the Number 7 bus to Fiesole—a village perched on a hill just north of Florence—along with other tourists and a few early-bird locals lugging shopping bags.

Gwen said it was a short ride past beautiful villas, only a half hour or so to the town square. If it wasn't too hot and they wanted to walk awhile, they could get out at the hamlet halfway between, she'd said, and enjoy the green hills. They do get out, peeking in first at the shadowy convent and church in tiny San Domenico.

They're breathless on the steep walk to Fiesole, May

trying not to limp, and she can't keep her thoughts from racing or her mind on the scenery, but it's turned into a beautiful day, and that helps. Liam was right that she belongs where it's green. Decadent Old Florence might be Gwen's kind of place and her mother's, but to May (and Liam, she's getting), it's like rich food: you can only eat so much before it makes you sick.

They enter the main square in Fiesole, park themselves on a bench, and stare down at the red-tiled rooftops of Florence, the cypress-specked hills of Mugello. There's a real breeze up here. The air smells clean, and swifts sweep past, diving in the open air high ahead. The two of them sit in comfortable silence: May processing the morning, Liam probably wondering what got her so upset. She isn't one to cry or panic, even in a crisis, and May can't remember the last time she's cried in front of anyone, least of all Li. He took it in stride, though, and she's grateful for that.

"Should we go to the Archaeological Museum?" he asks finally, his voice jarring in the silence. "Gwen'll kill us if we don't."

"I'm starved."

"Yeah, me too. Let's do lunch first and then walk."

The ancient Romans built a theater and baths up here, and according to the guidebook, here they are still, crumbling under the Tuscan skies. The ruins are just off the square, partly enclosed by cypress trees with descending hills visible beyond.

She and Liam are the only people inside the open park, and the hush is huge. There's something eerie and comforting about the orderly rows and stacks of stone, an outline of vanished lives.

"It's crazy"—Liam produces a thin blanket from his backpack, spreading it carefully, reading her mind—"that these things were built more than a thousand years before the Renaissance."

May gazes off at the ruins while Li finishes unpacking. The ragged rows are humbling, in a way. A sign on the way in said that there were Etruscan ruins here, too, dating back several hundred years *before* the Romans.

Cheese. Sliced apples. Olives. Crusty bread. "This here's all very Martha Stewart of you, Li. I'm impressed."

"You like?"

"I like," she says, tearing off a hunk of break to dab in the oil from the olives, then twisting the bread in her molars, chewing thoughtfully. "Do you ever think about how the past is always with us?"

"No."

"I'm serious," she says, swallowing. "I'm talking about my parents, the life we had as little kids. But way back before all that, too, before we were born. A bunch of people in togas walked around these ruins once, naming constellations and telling stories about Zeus and Hera."

"Who?"

She glares up at him again, and, again, he smiles. Of course he knows who Zeus and Hera are. Liam knows everything, probably. They're both academics' kids, spoon-fed this stuff, myths and histories, since before they could walk. It's only with grown-up life looming just out of the frame that May is grasping how little she knows, how none of it seems to add up.

"You're philosophical today."

May rips off another hunk of bread. "I've just been thinking how you can't stop it. The future's always coming at you like a train, and you can't see it to get out of the way."

"Yeah, but not all change is bad. Your parents are splitting," he ventures, "but they love you. They did their best all these years, and you're OK. You're like a grown-up now, and you have choices. They have to be able to choose, too."

"That's bullshit. You know it is."

"What? Which part?"

"'*They're splitting up but they love you.*' That's not the point. The point is they don't love *each other*, and that's not OK."

"Anymore," he adds firmly.

"Anymore," she echoes.

"Which isn't to say they didn't, or that your whole childhood was a lie, or any psych-shit like that."

In the same instant that May reaches out for more bread, Liam leans and tries to kiss her, almost missing her face completely. He grazes her cheekbone instead, and his lips feel wet and raw and surprising, not because Liam repels her—not that—but because he's Li, and Li isn't supposed to kiss her. "Whoa" is all she can say. *Whoa*.

Liam only looks at her, mortified probably, and May can't say what's worse, him hitting on her or him feeling embarrassed about it.

"Sorry," he mumbles. "Really bad timing. You were trying to say something—"

"Timing? Shit, Li. What are you doing?"

He looks sort of stunned, his face unnaturally red, and all she can think of is when they were about six and seven and for no discernible reason she threw sand in his face at the beach. She'd sat there with her hands in her wet lap while he howled about being blind. He hadn't cried but sort of gulped and stuck out his pudgy hands and groped the air, repeating his announcement—"*Blind, blind*"—in a small, vague voice as the waves rolled quietly over their legs and a seagull hovered on a current beside them, screaming. Finally Gwen (or was it Mom?) had seen him sitting there in his sagging fire-truck swim trunks, arms out in front of him like a deranged robot's, and came and brushed him off and walked him back to the blanket. Alone, May listened while the ocean murmured without judgment. It was soothing, just as the wind on this hilltop and the boundless blue Tuscan sky are now. *Sorry didn't do it*, the waves seemed to say, *but there are bigger things . . . bigger than him, bigger than you, bigger than now.*

Laced in with a feeling of excitement and curiosity about the morning's weirdness and the man she met is a kind of profound sadness that she can't explain to Liam, her childhood best friend. She would like to grab his arm and explain, to say that it won't always be like this, weird and wrong, that someday it will be like it was before, or some other, better way, but not *this* way.

But Li, whose hands are no longer pudgy—they're broad and long, with tapered fingers, she noticed when he was wiping away her tears—is already gone.

May sits a long while on his picnic blanket, feeling guilty, imagining he'll come back when he calms down. He'll come back when he's taken a breath or two, had a look over the rooftops below, had a minute to think.

But he doesn't, and at long last she cleans up those few scraps he didn't take with him and starts down the hill. She takes her own time getting back, doesn't want to arrive at the apartment before Gwen does, doesn't want to run into Li before Gwen can make things right again with cheerful updates on shroud-sucking vampires.

She bears right onto Via Vecchia Fiesolana, the old road, passing a tabernacle with a Madonna and Saints, and on the right, the church of Saint Jerome. Next is the Villa Medici. Yet another handy sign explains that the villa was built by Michelozzo in 1458 for Cosimo the Elder and used by Lorenzo the Magnificent to host his literary friends. Besides the beautiful gardens, which she meanders through absently, there isn't much remaining of the villa.

Heading out again, she reaches the terrace view that Queen Victoria liked so much she had her own bench installed there, and—was it left, now, or right . . . right—at the first intersection, the spot where the bishop of Fiesole, who lived in Florence, would rest on his way to his cathedral. *These people are all dead now,* May thinks with despair, circling back into San Domenico, with its church and convent, struggling out her phrase book so she can order a gelato in the shop across from the bus stop.

Ice cream is the only thing that makes sense anymore. This one's a rich hazelnut chocolate and tastes so good she lets the first Number 7 bus go by. It'll be a while before the next, an hour maybe. She knows that and just sits there taking long, slow licks like an animal cleaning its wound.

When she boards, she's the only passenger and watches wistfully, trying to hold on to the taste of chocolate as the landscape blurs past in a flicker of late-afternoon sunlight.

May slips back into the apartment and isn't surprised to find it empty. She settles on the overstuffed silky couch under the vaulted ceiling. That ceiling and the awesome terrace overlooking the Arno are the only real luxuries—the rest of the apartment is plain and modern; white stucco walls, terra-cotta tiled floors, a throw rug here and there. It's airy and light, and May feels just fine with that after visiting all those dank, dark churches yesterday, however beautiful their contents or contours. She picks up her novel from the coffee table and tries to read, but a clock somewhere in the still-strange house ticks ominously, and she can't concentrate.

Retreating to her room, May heads for the pile of research books on her desk, Gwen's mostly. "You have all these papers to write, so why not choose a topic that draws on where you are," Gwen advised, "or overlaps with the work I have you and Liam doing for me? Teachers — trust me; I am one — love visuals . . . the more, the better . . . so visit archives, take photos. Take advantage of this setting."

Yeah, but write about what? To crowd out the fact that she's possibly, probably, going insane, May closes her eyes, opens Gwen's copy of *Florence: An Encyclopedia* at random, stabs her forefinger down, and opens her eyes again.

Black Death (see also *Plague*).

Some lucky teacher's getting a paper on plague.

Medieval travelers carried home exotic cargo, money, and spices, she reads, surprisingly drawn in, *but also tales of terror and wonder.* May sits back down and cracks the book's spine in a way that would infuriate Gwen.

> At the hearthside or a packed table at the inn, they murmured of strange beasts and stranger men, of lands where dragons swept the skies, of seas swarming with monsters. To the average European — a peasant born into poverty and hardship — the places in travelers' tales seemed remote indeed.

> Rumors of calamity began to reach major trade centers like Florence as early as 1346, but, like unicorns and dragons, distant disaster was not of immediate concern. Merchants spoke of famine in the fabled East, of drought, floods, and swarming locusts. They told of earthquakes bringing down mountains, enormous hailstones battering the earth, of fire raining down "in flakes like snow" from skies that might as easily bring storms of serpents, frogs, and scorpions. Worst of all was an infected wind, one so poisonous you could see it—a vicious, stinking smoke. Any who breathed this smoke dropped dead in the space of a day. This wind had mowed down millions, and there were fearful rumors of its progress.

Lifting the book, May snatches a notebook and pencil from the desk, then pads in bare feet out to the terrace, her favorite part of the apartment. From there she can look out over the rooftops at the edge of the city, which butt right up to the wide Arno, with its ancient bridges and green hills beyond. She settles into an iron chair beside a planter, with her feet on the railing, enjoying the sun on her face a moment, and reads on.

According to the book, the outbreak that people of Cristofana's day called the pestilence or the Pest, which was formerly confined to the Far East, now began to fan out in different directions, tearing through Indian Tartary, Mesopotamia, and Syria, and settling in the Tartar lands of Asia Minor in 1346, where it left 85,000 dead in Crimea alone.

In the chaos, the Tartars seized the chance to launch a campaign against Genoese merchants at a trading base in Tana. They chased their quarry to Caffa, another fortified Genoese trading center on the Crimean coast, pitched camp outside the city walls, and got ready to bombard Caffa into submission, but the Tartar invaders didn't figure plague into their strategy. It locked on with a vengeance, leveling their ranks. Those left standing moved to retreat, but first the Tartars gave the Genoese a taste of their woe. Using giant catapults, they lobbed the corpses of their fellows over Caffa's walls.

May lifts her pencil and scrawls BIOLOGICAL WARFARE across the top of the first blank page in the notebook, underlining it three times. There. She'll compare the way the Black Death arrived in Europe to modern forms of biological warfare. Her world history teacher will love it.

She looks up when she hears the front door of the

apartment open, her heart racing when she deduces from the tread that it isn't Gwen. May left the terrace doors open, so he'd know she was out here, but Liam retreats without a word, first into the bathroom and then to his own tiny bedroom at the far end of the apartment, beside hers, and through his closed door she hears the musical lilt of his laptop firing up.

This Too Shall Pass

Following Gwen from arch to nook to nave in search of the day's reliquary weirdness, May tries to crowd the artist, an enigma, out of her mind and focus instead on Cristofana, on the problem of time. But in May's world, it's Liam, who's Princeton-bound and actually *wants* to study physics, who does the supersize cosmic thinking, and he's been glued to his text screen all day, scowling over it, his thumbs roving the keyboard whenever he has service.

May seems to have alienated the only person she would even dream of telling.

She half remembers her dad talking about some theory proposed a few years ago at MIT or someplace, about time existing in slices like bread, all lined up to make a loaf. And sometimes the slices shift and overlap, and you aren't here anymore — you're there — and there are wormholes between. Or something. God, she should have paid attention.

Liam, across the room, looks up and away again.

Why didn't she pay more attention — to everything, the good things — while she could? Before they were gone and there were these choices to make. Before everything changed. *Why can't things just stay the same?*

May must have said something out loud, because Gwen gives her a look that promises, *Hold that thought*, bringing a finger to her lips. *Hush*.

They are in the quietest, dimmest, grimmest church they've been in all day — which is saying a lot — in search of the remains of Saint Juliana Falconieri, which turn out to be in an ornate glass box edged in filigreed gold under a side altar. The leaflet May thumbs through says that the body, Juliana's, is incorrupt. But Gwen points out (to May only, since Liam keeps to the opposite side of whatever echo-filled room they find themselves in, squinting at his blue screen) that a mask has been applied to her face and hands, so who knows.

Another body, preserved under an altar in another

church, was well preserved and never decayed or discolored, even though that saint died in 1459.

Next up is the habit worn by Saint Francis when he received the stigmata, preserved in the church of Ognissanti, which puts May over the top. "Remind me why we're doing this?" she mutters.

May's seventeen years old, barely out of the starting gate, and spending her summer surrounded by corpses and remains. Yet she's rarely felt so alive as she did looking into the liquid darkness of that artist's eyes.

They were doing this because May made the mistake of asking what relics were, after seeing the term one too many times in her guidebook, which lit the bulb over Gwen's egghead and got her planning and phoning all over the city, vowing, "I'll show you. I have a few stops to make anyway."

Gwen explained that in medieval Europe, people swore by the magical properties of saints, holding even their skin and bones in awe. Their bodies were considered superhuman. A dead saint might be ripped to shreds by faithful Christians seeking miraculous healing. Every boot, bone, and strand of hair was whisked away for the sick and needy, with not a tooth or a scrap of robe remaining. Blood was drained from the bodies or blotted up in garments to soak up luck and protection.

Corpses of famous saints were taken apart and divvied up among rival churches, which put these relics on display or paraded them around to improve morale in bad times. Churches even stole from competing parishes to boost their reputations. "The tongues of a handful of saints were said to remain preserved," Gwen explained, "long after their bodies had decayed. Saint Anthony of Padua's was billed as 'red, soft, and entire' more than four hundred years after he died."

May looked at Liam when Gwen made the tongue comment, smiling in solidarity, but he refused to meet her eyes.

Oh, right. We're not speaking.

Every so often, she catches him looking back with those stark blue eyes. He's a good-looking guy, with that jaw and that dark stubble with a sheen of red mixed in, that wide-shouldered frame and crooked smile, with that way he has, when the phone's in his pocket, at least, of thoughtfully trailing his fingers over the things they pass, every stone, as if to register its temperature. All this makes her wonder why she didn't just let him kiss her in Fiesole. Would life be easier if she had? Would she feel less alone?

Right now she isn't allowing herself to feel much of anything *except* alone. May feels off, wrong, not quite healthy or *here* somehow. Maybe all this weirdness is only May hallucinating herself into some other moment in history and back again, but isn't that worth a worry? Shouldn't she be *doing* something about it? To fix herself if she's broken?

Why did those people do it? she thinks, peering in at reliquaries under their spotlights. *Tear their heroes limb from limb?* Is it because she's so ordinary that none of this seems real enough to startle or penetrate? Good old normal May . . . unexceptional except in the right and approved ways—straight A's, or nearly straight—uncomplicated in her demands. What did she have to lose? What would she tear a body limb from limb for? She has no trouble at all imagining her witchy twin tearing a corpse to bits, but the phenomenon of Cristofana doesn't feel like something to unveil to Gwen and Liam over antipasto.

If only she could trust her own thoughts, so jangled and unreal, to know the difference between real and not real anymore, but even Liam isn't the Liam she knew. How can she trust a world so changed . . . or so quickly changing?

This time when she looks for Li, he looks back, only for a second—with regret and defensiveness in his eyes—and May concludes that no matter how needy you are, there's always someone else . . . always others . . . needing, too. That's just how it is. She'll keep her problems to herself.

"Why did they do it?" she finally asks aloud, sidling close to Gwen, who regards her with concern.

"Do what?"

"Tear their saints apart like that? It's such a savage way to . . . get help. It isn't very Christian, to say the least." Did the artist in Old Florence believe in superstitions like that? The thought made her sad, more than anything, though it wasn't sadness she associated with him. Every time the young man from the workshop entered her thoughts, May felt an excitement she had no name for, a dark thrill and a promise. A promise that life would break, probably, because it—the promise, but life, too—made no sense.

"Blood magic seemed very real and present in those times. But even more recently, people dug up and stole the skulls of great composers, hoping for a clue to their genius. Einstein donated his own brain for postmortem study—even though some of it ended up filed away in a dusty cider carton in some doctor's office. Then there are cryonics and other efforts to 'miraculously' preserve the body with hopes of reanimating it later. And think of all we've learned from genetics."

May peers in at poor Saint Juliana in her ghastly mask, half expecting her to comment.

They walk to another section of the chapel, which Gwen calls the friary. In one of its frescoes, people and cows lie swollen and obviously dead. The leaflet says that the fresco was in tribute to the 63,000 lives lost in Florence during the Great Mortality.

"I'm going to write one of my papers about the plague, I've decided. What year was it here?"

Gwen lifts her eyebrows. "Which one? It's cyclical, unfortunately."

"The big one." May points to the frescoes.

"The Black Death. Fourteenth century—1348, I think."

Conscious of Liam's irritation—she can almost hear him thinking, *Don't get her going again*—of Gwen looking from Liam to her and back again, curiously, noticing for the first time, perhaps, that they haven't spoken all day, haven't joked or shoved or whispered in rebellion against her edu-tyranny, May kneels to study the bottom half of the frescoes, which mostly depict religious scenes, but a few show farmers in the field, people gathered in a courtyard, ordinary people.

Gwen kneels, too, and together they stare silently ahead. "Things never do stay the same, May. Look at these frescoes. Every one of these people is gone now. . . ."

"They're beautiful, though," she murmurs, one hand hovering over the fading paint (she knows better than to touch), thinking of the artist, half smiling in secret, because for the first time she has someone to obsess over, to pine after, to feel ridiculous for.

"You're more like your mother than you think." Gwen stands up, brightening. "Would you two like to see how it's done? I know a painter who gives demonstrations in his studio. . . ."

Suspending animosity for the moment, May and Liam groan in tandem and head for the exit.

There is only one painter May wants to see.

We Correspond

After a week of sightseeing and glutting out on Italian food, May almost forgets Cristofana, forgets to believe or disbelieve. Except for the persistent—if impossible—memory of the artist, she becomes a mindless tourist again, following Gwen from one cultural treasure to another or running errands for the book she and Liam are supposed to be helping with. Even a modest ambition, like luring Li into a bout of thumb wrestling over antipasto (when he's more or less mastered the art of not looking at her), seems beyond her.

So, before their afternoons out and dinner, she takes to the terrace to get some work done, or try to; as Gwen reminds her daily, her essays aren't going to write themselves.

So far she's only taken notes, but this morning she has the apartment to herself, and May's determined to write at least an outline. It isn't much, but it's a beginning, and she has to begin.

She heads to Gwen's office corner in the front room and starts piling up books, meaning to bring them out to the terrace, where her tea and biscotti are already waiting, but as she passes her own room, something makes her pause. May listens without moving, without breathing, her arms sagging with books, and nudges the door with her big toe.

Why isn't she surprised, she wonders, to find a ghosted-out Cristofana reclining comfortably on her bed, admiring her faint self in the mirror?

May's almost amused at first, relieved that it wasn't an intruder in there, but then again, it *is* an intruder, and she feels her relief darken. "Don't you believe in knocking?"

Cristofana seems hurt, turning her haughty gaze back to her own reflection, and May almost feels for her. It's uncanny and deeply disturbing—how physically alike they are, despite their different forms, one flesh and one phantom—but the resemblance is skin-deep only, and May knows better than to trust a thing just because it's familiar.

Besides which, with Cristofana right in front of her, real enough to almost (if pointlessly) touch, it's all rushing back now, the reality of what she's been through since she got here, along with that dark thrill, that impossible promise that maybe isn't impossible after all. What if she *can* see the man in the artists' workshop again? For a second May has to close her eyes, overcome by the memory of his hands and how he smelled.

First things first, she thinks. "You need to explain something to me," she says aloud.

Cristofana nods. She must understand that she has May on the hook, and she's not rushing.

"You said you were looking for me. But *why*? I mean, why me? There had to have been others you—?"

"Yes, but none so similar in aspect. None so like me. Time does not allow for trade unless the trade is even, a nose for a nose, a hand for a hand." She finally looks up, right into May's eyes with her negative-but-identical ones. "We correspond."

"You mean genetics . . . DNA? Are you saying we're related?" May's mother had tried to get her interested in genealogy before the trip. "*We have people from Italy, you know, generations ago. I have a picture of your great-grandmother somewhere. She was from a seaside village on a cliff*—*Corniglia, I think.*" May, in no mood to think about family new or old, had politely changed the subject.

"I have no knowledge of this," Cristofana replies. "Related?"

"Are we family?" The last thing May wants is more family right now. More choices. More regrets.

"I have no family," her twin replies coldly, and May can see that it's a sore subject for her; maybe they do have a thing or two in common, besides their appearance.

Cristofana rises lazily, stretches like a cat, and crosses to the desk. She peers down at yesterday's debris: pens and highlighters . . . crumbs, snack plates, and empty teacups . . . the already-scoured research texts. "You have a great many books."

"For what it's worth. None of them are helping me get my essay written. I have enough notes to write a book of my own—"

"Essays?"

"For school."

"You attend school? Like highborn men? Your family is very wealthy?"

"Listen. Maybe we should cut to the chase here.

Before someone comes home and hears me talking to myself." *It's a moot point*, May thinks, since you can't really see her out in the sunlight. "Why are you here today? Again."

"I have more to show you." She looks hungrily, almost furtively, around the room and then out the tall arched window offering a sliver view of rooftops, with the dome and campanile jutting out above it all. "You will come back with me?"

If she could trust this girl, it might be worth the risk, to find him again, to know him better than she imagines she already does. On the other hand, that's a big "if," and the Middle Ages are a truly scary place. "I might," she relents. "Later. If I decide I can trust you."

"You *will* return—I know it—and you won't be sorry. I have much to show you. There are dancing bears here in your world, at market, and jugglers?"

"I'm more of an art person myself," May quips, but the joke falls on deaf ears. "No. We have malls," she says, "and television. I suppose that counts."

"What is television?"

"Never mind that now." May gets up, and Cristofana follows her out to the terrace. The girl leans over the shaded stone railing and stares left and then right, making dizzy noises in her throat like a child going too high too fast on a swing.

"From where does it all come?" she muses, and May can't answer, can't begin to comprehend how changed everything must look to Cristofana. On the other hand, remembering the pared-down version of Florence Past, she *can* imagine. Either way — more, less — the shift is a shock, a miracle of sorts.

"Shouldn't you get inside? Someone might see you from the street or a window and wonder what's up." Suddenly May wants very much to be away from Cristofana; she wants to think without her influence — to delay this and all decisions — *think*, *think*, but her double's voice jars her. May continues, "At least move out of the shade." What May can make out of Cristofana in this bright light is staring down at the patio table, at May's notes on the progress of the plague.

She's been reading all this time, and her tone is eerie and remote, as if she's in a trance. "Can you not imagine it, *bella*? Standing at the base of a sturdy stone wall, savage cries all surrounded, when a corpse comes hurtling from the heavens with your name on its lips?"

May gapes. "What are you talking about?"

The girl looks up as if startled. "Filthy Tartars. But enough now of such fearsome stuff. Are you ready to go? I will not return or extend this invitation again."

May absently fans the pages of one of the research books, trying not to fathom the paralyzing boredom she'll feel if she does the right thing, the safe thing . . . if she says no.

Without a word, she closes the book and circles back inside. Rifling through her wardrobe, she assembles the plainest outfit she can find—a long sack-like T-shirt dress, faded brown, with three-quarter sleeves . . . leather sandals . . . *just call me* Friar *Tuck*—and changes quickly. "Let's go," she calls to the barely there girl on the terrace, and holds the front door open.

Nothing in the past seems different, at first.

May follows Cristofana and the clamor of voices and cart wheels to the market square. There is the same long, columned, rectangular piazza skirted by stone towers, the same wooden stalls and merchant stands, the same men in capes and women with their wares spread on blankets or piled in baskets. But there are fewer stalls, fewer wares, and fewer people picking through them. The minute May sees the crowd, she hangs back. "They can't see you," her twin reassures her. It seems to take shade and shadows, dark backdrops, to provide contrast. May saw for herself how Cristofana effectively vanished on the bright terrace but was as obvious as day indoors. "Stay out in the white light, and you will be fine. If one should glimpse you, as I have said, you will seem a phantom, and he will doubt his own mind."

May moves reluctantly forward, and it's true that no one seems to register her presence as she passes, but there's also a strange watchfulness in everyone's eyes — expectancy, even terror. May feels both invisible and exposed. If they *could* see her, she thinks, their eyes would pick her apart like starving animals at a carcass. They all seem to be waiting for something.

May has the hollow, headachy feeling again, and the nausea, and intermittently her ears feel full of cotton. She might be the only one moving in the whole square, until a figure in an overhanging window dumps down a bucket of foul-looking water, missing her by a foot, making her jump. *Not that it matters*, May thinks. *I wouldn't feel it.*

She crosses into a partitioned stall arranged with bolts of fabric and hanging leather goods, catching her own warped, barely there reflection in a tall glass bottle. It strikes her, looking around, how few reflective surfaces there are in Old Florence, where everything is wood and stone and straw. She's startled by a horse and wagon *clop-clopping* behind her, the driver whipping the poor animal into a frenzy. She winces, covering her ears against the sounds of the whip connecting with flesh, of the animal whinnying in complaint. May looks over at Cristofana. It's especially weird to be here with her double in the flesh, even more like looking in a mirror. While they wait for the cart to pass, May says, "Have I mentioned that I still don't believe in you?"

"Very funny, *bella*. Ha. But I believe in you, and that is all that matters, since here you are. You have florin, yes?" The cart finally passes, and Cristofana moves forward abruptly, smoothing her tangle of dark-blond hair and her dress, which is gray, like her—*their*—eyes, and which trails on the ground. She waves her hand dismissively, remembering. She speaks under her breath, since as far as those around her are concerned, she's alone. "Even if you do, your ghost coins will not profit me, but see here what lovely wares they have left to sell?"

Cristofana stops to let May take it all in, and then she extends her palm, where one gold coin shines dully. "I have stolen this, you see, from the home of the wealthy merchant who took me into service. This is why I must now keep to the shadows, though you must not. His other servants will not spy me because he has none. They have all fled, though his wife clings to her fine ways with all her might, and I am forever dressing and undressing her and plaiting her hair just so. She is probably croaking for me now, calling from her big bed for me to fetch the leech. She is not sick, my mistress, but her wealthy friends bring terrible rumors, and I think she wills herself sick to end the suspense. For her, suspense is worse than death." Again, that waving hand. "Look here: mallow, nettles, mercury plant. Herbs for drawing abscesses. They'll serve when the pestilence comes. Soon they will be hard to find. . . ."

"I have no idea what you're talking about." May wants to get the upper hand, wants a word in edgewise.

"*Bella*, I talk, watch, listen — do all this — magnificently. I also sing and steal. My father was a *pirata*." She taps her forehead. "I have his sea songs here. My English mother was a whore with a virgin's eyes, and I have her gifts, too."

Be proud, May thinks, *very proud*, but the question begs asking. "So you have no family left?"

"My parents are dead, and good riddance. I was raised by wolves with Saint Francis as my saint. My given name is Frances, though I adopted Cristofana from a girl I once robbed. I stole her name and her ring finger, too, when she wouldn't do as I asked and remove her ruby." Cristofana displays a monstrous ring, flashing it so briefly that May can hardly make it out.

"You're lying, aren't you?" Somehow, already, May knows those rhythms of speech, that lilting intonation, the glint in those eyes, as if she's known them always.

"Do you deserve the truth?"

A clamor nearby distracts May before she can answer — *doesn't everyone?* — a ragged man shouting on a step, and when Frances or Cristofana or whoever she is sees him, she moves fast, stepping close. "He brings a crowd," she whispers, "and maybe my master."

Drawn closer to the shadowy edges of the market by her quite possibly insane guide, May keeps to open sunlight, walking through anything in her path, and it's a good thing, because she wouldn't be able to keep up otherwise; Cristofana moves nimbly, easily navigating stalls, wooden wheelbarrows, pigs, prancing roosters, and the man kneeling on the cobbles by the cow he's just butchered, surrounded by meat, offal, and flies. May fights a big wave of nausea.

"They're at market every day now, these wandering preachers, ranting about the doomsday. But this one's a true prophet, they say, a holy man who lived alone in a cave in the wilderness. He survived on berries and roots and wild boar he trapped and killed with his bare hands. Monks in the hills brought him barley bread and beans."

With the man has come a whole discordant parade.

Small boys bang on drums and clang cymbals. Women stoop and wail. Seeing the confusion in her eyes when the Italian sermon begins, Cristofana repeats the man's every word in a near whisper, translating deftly. "Death is come across the ocean," he's shouting, "dealing pestilence. This city has for too long offended God. It will burn like the sinful cities of Sodom and Gomorrah. Even now, Death is scything its way here on ships loaded with dainties and delicacies, shameless trinkets brought from the godless lands of the infidels in the East to indulge the vices of the rich. Death will pluck them from their scented baths and plant them in narrow pits and make of them a feast for worms. I saw under the altar of souls them that were slain for the word of God."

"Come with me," Cristofana says, leaning, "and I will show you the way this world is going. When next you return, I may be gone. We all may be."

May finally makes the connection. Alarms sound in her sluggish brain. One of the first things Cristofana said to her the other time they visited this market, the time her double slipped through the portal and swapped worlds with her, without permission, was, *Long ago, in the year of our Lord 1347, I caught a sparrow in my hands. . . .*

"What's the date?" May whispers, and the horror must echo out in her voice.

Cristofana studies her with interest. "Date?"

"Today. What year is it? What month?"

The howling preacher interrupts as if on cue. "There shall be famine, and pestilence, and earthquakes in diverse places. These are the beginnings of sorrows."

Cristofana sets off without answering, and May hurries after, searching the empty gazes of helpless, milling strangers and instinctively trying to avoid mangy chickens fleeing underfoot, and drovers and cattle flowing past in a crooked line, though she needn't bother. None of them know she's here. No one does. Not Liam, not Gwen. Not her parents. Just Cristofana.

"The arches of the shops on the street are rented out to the wealthiest merchants," says her guide, "but these have already left the city."

May glances inside at shadowy bolts of fabric and diseased-looking sausage links and sides of ham, swathed in flies, dangling in the windows; she tries to beat back her panic.

"That man over there had wax amulets last week, made from Easter candles blessed by the pope. He'll sell you pardons for your sins, salvation for every size purse. He has these on parchment, sacred documents fresh from Rome signed by cardinals or the pope himself. He has also the cheap stuff approved by mere bishops, priors, and archdeacons.

"For a fee, the same man will consent for you to glimpse the holy relics in his pockets, brought here by providence. He'll narrate their arduous journey from the Holy Land centuries ago here to the streets of Firenze, guided by God's own hand. A truer miracle never was, he'll say.

"As for me," she whispers, "I have seen enough wood from Christ's cross to build Noah's ark. But so great is this city's fear of being struck down in a state of sin, who would scoff at divine protection? Do you see their faces? They believe, with all their hearts, and they are helpless."

Again, the itinerant preacher hoarsely punctuates Cristofana's words. "And I looked, and beheld a pale horse: and his name that sat upon him was Death, and Hell followed with him. . . . For the great day of his wrath is come; and who shall be able to stand? . . . This was prophesied, and this has come to pass."

The holy man's eyes are hollow and filmy and make May shudder. The drummer boys are marching to and fro, smiling, as if this is all one big Sunday parade.

Cristofana pauses by the preacher and his entourage. She's on a mission, it seems, and there's no stopping or silencing her.

"It's not only men with cures for the soul who warn," she says, "but those who trade and travel. Merchants and the men who drive animals to the distant markets, these all speak of bandits raiding their carts, of cheap and abandoned goods, of multitudes leading teams of horses with bulging packs away from the towns. The words you penned on your paper book—"

"Are you saying you understood them . . . my notes about plague?"

"In your scholar *essay*?" she says coyly. "Yes. I've said that my mother was English—herself the child of a great scholar. She taught me to read to spite Papa." She leaves the bigger question of comprehension, of understanding what she read and of what it means in this moment, this lifetime, unanswered. Unanswerable. "Your words are confirmed now every day in the streets of Firenze. It's whispered that each and every rotten corpse the Tartars flung over their walls, the Genoese lifted like a clumsy log. They jogged their ugly, unwanted gifts through town and—heave-ho—hurled them into the harbor. But how will a besieged city fight an enemy within as well as without? Soon the pestilence awoke inside Caffa's walls. The survivors took to their ships. They sailed for the Mediterranean, to Messina and Genoa, bringing their burden with them.

"The Great Mortality moves just so over land and sea. It is moving as we speak. The truth is right here at market. Look." Cristofana waves May over near a girl with a basket, who flinches to hear Cristofana murmuring, seemingly, to herself, but then Cristofana turns her attention almost immediately, hypnotically, back to the preacher. "Usually, her basket is overflowing. All along this wall, she and other girls would stand competing with the clamor of tough old birds, women who sell the dried chestnuts, cheese, and mustard seeds — all manner of good things to make vegetable flans and pies and ravioli with. You see, there are no more craftsmen or wool and flax dealers, either . . . and only the one butcher. Even the dice players and the moneylenders with their green cloth tables are gone. Everyone hoards food and charges too much. To succeed at market now, you must be a purveyor of medical, magical, and spiritual protection against sickness. You must sell potions, like that man over there. He carries the best pottery and bone charms."

Cristofana begins threading her way through the crowd again, and May, lost and otherwise in thrall by terror, follows obediently, looking wherever her guide motions. "It is God's will that medicine will be effective only if taken by a blameless person, but now the holy men are upstaged when a leech or a cunning woman lays out a table with protective charms and potions. My own lady swears by them and spends every florin she has to save her hide as well as her soul."

Cristofana stops in her tracks, turning. She leans close and whispers with violent intensity, "I care little for my soul, *bella*. I love my body. I love my sharp eyes, my knowing nose, my clever hands." She lets those hands hover intently over May's ghost shoulders, staring into faint, transfixed eyes.

We correspond.

"I do not wish to die. Not for Heaven's sake or any other." The hands fall to her sides. "You will help me?"

In a split second, May tears her gaze away, remembering the closing words of the chapter she was copying out before Cristofana showed up that morning: *Before it was over, between one-eighth and one-half of the population of Europe would fall down dead with plague.*

She bolts, running as fast as she can — it feels like flying with no obstructions, nothing to contain her but gravity — retracing her crooked, crowded path to the alley behind the abandoned shop, and the sideways 8, and the relief of an invisible exit.

Keep Your Enemies Close

The last thing in the world May wants is to go back. Ever. But her better judgment erodes quickly.

With so many questions and only Cristofana to answer them, May stops sleeping through the night. She stares at the ceiling in the dark. She tosses and turns, and her mind and body ring with waiting.

The trouble is that Time Present—even among supportive (if complicated, in Liam's case) friends in a magnificent city like Florence—pales right now in the deep, dark shadow of Time Past. Her brush with Old

Florence, the intrigues of a crazy girl wearing her face and flesh, the historic enormity of the Black Death, and her meeting with the beautiful artist — not to mention what the plague means for him and others like him — all begins to rule May's every sensible thought and impulse.

If Gwen and Liam have noticed any odd behavior on her part, they don't speak of it. They seem to get that May needs space, and they let her be preoccupied when she has to be.

Who was he, and would he survive?

Without benefit of words or manners, without intrusion or fumbling, the artist in Old Florence seemed to see right into May as if he knew a secret shortcut to her soul. In moments, he thrilled her senses and made every fiber of her feel greedy and alive with *now*, and yet he isn't here *now* . . . and how would May ever find him again, and warn him, if she didn't go back? If Cristofana didn't invite her back.

The sketch on the artist's easel, terrible and beautiful at once, is as much a mystery as he is. Thanks to all the reading she's been doing and her tourist treks with Gwen, May knows that the image she saw and can't forget — one suggesting the artist may not need a warning, that he's well aware of what's coming — very likely has no (surviving) precedent from his own day.

Before and during the Renaissance, artwork was commissioned either by the Church or by powerful patrons who dictated style and subject matter. There was nothing gothic or strange or surreal about it. Maybe May's mystery man was a stranger in his day just as she was.

May tells herself that her obsession with going back has a practical side. If she can find a way to disable the portal, her double and the plague (and even the artist, if that's what it takes to stay safe) might all slip away into a mist of disbelief.

It makes sense, after all, that Cristofana, a self-professed orphan with nothing and no one to lose in her own world, wants a way out of Hell—the Black Death is about to rip through her Florence and level everyone in its path—and this is something May can't give her without losing everything. But on the other hand, sensibly speaking, if May doesn't figure out how to close the portal for good, she'll live in dread. She'll go through the summer—her life, possibly—looking over her shoulder.

But as of now, if the invisible passage is going to open again, only Cristofana can open it, and it may be that only she can close it again, and keep it closed.

Keep your friends close, May's always heard, *but your enemies closer*, and for the first time those words make sense. But how can she affect anything if she doesn't even know what Cristofana *is*? Her twin isn't a ghost. She may look like one, at least in May's world, and sure, she's dead — literally speaking — has to be, since she lived in some other century (if not dead, then certainly *past*), but May has seen with her own eyes that Cristofana's Florence, that timescape, for lack of a better word, still exists, just not *now*.

Cristofana exists *in it*, and so does the man in the workshop.

Her twin has a portable doorway and crosses through it, moving back and forth; she even brought May through, back to some moment in the Middle Ages, which is hardly the point May or any sane person would dial to if they had their own personal time machine, because it's dark and filthy, full of funk and disease, and hard for women especially, or so May is reading, so she was taught in school. All this she knows. But what does she really know?

Pull one small stitch from an old tapestry, or from time, and it becomes something else. The picture alters. The outcome changes.

Almost two weeks later, Cristofana comes for her, and May can't help it. She goes willingly, drawn as if by invisible threads. May might be the specter in this place, but it's her twin acting like the Ghost of

Christmas Future from that Charles Dickens story, all drawn eyes and doomy gestures and pointing. She moves with her usual stealth and speed, though, and May can hardly keep up on her macabre tour of a changed city.

They visit abandoned shops, basement hovels full of rain and echoes, and once-grand villas where dirty men and boys recline on beds of filthy straw. These squatters whisper to Cristofana in lewd voices or try to touch her as she passes, though she evades them easily. They're too weak and demoralized to exert themselves, and they rarely notice the baffled shadow in an Old Navy dress and leather sandals behind her. Most people don't see the figment that is May . . . or don't believe their eyes if they do.

Because these squatters light cooking fires on the floors, the once-beautiful drapes and paintings in these homes are black with soot. Some villas, Cristofana warns, are barred and well guarded. Their noble inhabitants — those who haven't already fled to the countryside — dress and dine as they always have. With their backs straight, they play the lute and tell tales and pretend the world outside is gone.

Following, at the edge of her nerves, May tries to work out a way to ask the question that's dogged her since Cristofana turned up: *Where is he?* She has no idea how to find the artists' quarter on her own, though she does recognize in passing certain stern towers hemming in the cobble streets, towers that still exist in Florence Present.

May can't stop thinking about the man, even or perhaps especially, anxiously, in the midst of Cristofana's tour of horrors. His face keeps looping through her thoughts, distracting from her mission, which is ostensibly to figure out how the portal works and disable it, protect or seal herself off from Cristofana once and for all. She feels like what she used to accuse Sarah and Jenna back home of being when they let their boyfriends or would-be/should-be boyfriends cloud their brains, let attractions get in the way of everything—school, friendship, family, the world—idiotic and self-absorbed. What does it say about her that she's here on a guided tour of Hell, with no thought but his eyes, his hands? If it's some escapist thing, she can't help it. She can't stop.

But to ask after him, to give Cristofana that much insight into her, is to give her too much. So May bites her tongue as her twin marches her past barren fields beyond the city, where farm animals wander blankly in the tall grass, untended; past foreign flagellants parading between the towers in deserted streets, whipping their bare backs with knotted cords, splashing blood, chanting psalms, promising the end of the world.

When May finally pleads, "What do you want from me, Cristofana? Why are you showing me all this?" the other girl won't answer, only looks back with those knowing eyes, familiar and strange—the trick of a fun-house mirror. One minute her expression is bleak and distant; the next it's full of winking menace. May is afraid of her, but not too afraid to feel intrigued or, as now, impatient. "If there's nothing we can do, why am I here?"

"I ask myself this every day, *bella*. And why should you have an answer, when I do not?"

Their next stop is the villa of Cristofana's rich employer and his wife. Both have recently died, which seems to come as no surprise to her. The house is hushed and full of flies. Looking around furtively, Cristofana partially closes the door to the bedroom where husband and wife lie blotched and bloated in their paneled bed. She begins rifling through trunks in the hallway, toying with the lady's silks and feathers and finery, a litter of hungry kittens circling her ankles.

"Can't we do anything for them?" May repeats,

motioning toward the half-closed door, behind which the prostrate pair looks anything but serene in death. The smell in here is overpowering, and for a moment May has to fight off real nausea, above and beyond the queasiness of being ghosted in the past. It's a weird sensation, since whatever's in her stomach has to be incorporeal like the rest of her; she can no more vomit here than touch or taste. "Can't we bring someone for them?" she pleads.

"There is no one."

Cristofana has already explained that the priests and doctors are mostly dead themselves, that those left standing will not enter a plague house wherein there are no sick left to save.

"The human dead are no more in our thoughts," she declares, waving a hand, "than dead goats. And if we draw attention, it will only bring the *bechini*." She waves toward the bedroom. "They'll rob my master's heirs and rape me, given the chance." She looks up, her eyes vacant a moment, sensing May's question. Cristofana always reels a question from the silence long before May knows to ask it. "The *bechini* are criminals, men condemned to man the oars of galley ships. When they offered to help bury the dead, they were set free. And now they roam like the ravenous wolves that circle the city walls at night, smelling death. Like fools, we threw the gates wide open. There. That is the trunk I want."

Cristofana herds the needy kittens away with her foot, holding another key up to the scant light penetrating heavy drapes. The lock makes a satisfying *clunk*. She begins to root through the trunk, twining herself in a beautifully crafted shawl. "They say women are too free now, whores, every one." She holds up her arm to admire the embroidery. "That society no more knows right from wrong or evil from otherwise. They let a woman wear her hair flowing and her bodice cinched, and they don't blink when she lifts her skirts to cross the mud. Look at you." She laughs. "Your legs. Could they see you, this would have shocked and horrified. Today not so much. The wealthy hire in musicians . . . they called me in once to sing . . . they let a woman sing now. When the widows are sick—like the mother of my mistress when her children forsook her—they let their male servants tend to them and touch them, because they have no one else."

"You're the one who should think about what you're touching," May says. "For example . . . *that*?" She points at the shawl and the pile of clothing belonging to the dead woman. "It's contagious, you know, this sickness, horribly. Do you know what *contagious* means?"

"Afraid?" Cristofana lets one of the kittens sidle up her embroidered arm, where it purrs into her neck. "Do you not think it fate? Our hour of dying?"

The kitten's fur is dull, a greasy gray over a thin frame, but it's too young not to hope. Its eyes brim with it.

Cristofana offers a velvet cape from the next trunk, her eyes expectant. "You won't play? Perhaps you see such fine things every day where you come from?"

"Thank you, no." May sighs, sick with dread and exasperated. She isn't about to get into the details of pandemic and public health when Cristofana and her whole generation haven't even mastered basic hygiene. Irrationally, May almost smiles, imagining her double squaring off against Ms. Bestle in health class.

Cristofana drapes the cape over her arm and sprays herself with perfume from an ornate bottle. It's Venetian glass, or at least looks like one of the bottles May almost bought for her mom in the market. The smell seems to inspire Cristofana. All of a sudden she's twirling in her borrowed garments, in silk and velvet and feathers, humming madly under her breath.

One of the kittens teeters on Cristofana's shoulder, its paws kneading at the shawl, and May imagines herself moving in such layers, of the artist considering her in them, which is kind of ridiculous, really. She can't remember the last time she wore anything but jeans or shorts or a skirt and T. What would a man like that, trained to see beauty, make of her typical wardrobe and her long, wild dirty-blond hair tied back in a scrunchie? Would he even give her a second look? She almost wishes she could get the blue gown back, the one she stole from a clothesline and left abandoned in the alley by the portal.

He already has, May thinks — again with that secret smile. *More than one*.

The would-be center of attention is not amused. "It can't harm you," Cristofana complains, examining the green velvet cape and flinging it away like a striptease artist. She sets down the kitten before adjusting her remaining layers, leaving her own clothing, rags mostly, in a puddle at her feet. She scoops up the animal again and with a sigh of scorn spits on the pile.

May follows her out through eerie, deserted rooms with high ceilings and secretive hangings. They move without a sound.

She can't understand why the streets are so quiet until it occurs to her that there are no bells ringing. Every other time she's been here, there were church bells tolling almost constantly in the background, too regular to take note of. They tolled for the dead, Cristofana has explained. They were a record of the taken. Is everyone dead now? How long has she been away? Is the artist dead? she wonders, seized by terror. Did he survive these early weeks of the plague? "Where are the bells?"

Cristofana tilts her head thoughtfully, closing her eyes to enjoy the softness of the little cat nuzzling her ear. "The officials forbade them. . . . Too much ringing. Too much despair."

"It's *too* quiet now."

Cristofana looks deflated suddenly, broken, and since May has never seen her twin reveal any emotion at all beyond a kind of ruthless curiosity, she can only stare, which seems to snap her double out of it. "Most of the shops have closed," she adds haughtily, as if this explains everything.

A deafening commotion a street away rivets her double's attention. Hurrying to a gap between buildings, Cristofana turns down the narrow walkway, veers a moment midway, the kitten swaying on her shoulder, and disappears into the chaos and glare on the opposite side.

May can just make out a group of onlookers over there by the street, surging toward an even bigger crowd passing in the roadway, wailing in grief and lamentation.

Her eyes lock on a shape in deep shadow by one of the walls between the buildings. A dog, she thinks at first, or some other animal nosing for food scraps, but when the figure starts shrieking and writhing in pain, she realizes it's a man slumped on the cobbles.

"He begs," Cristofana says, reemerging to his right—translating in that obliging way of hers and not bothering to whisper in passing—"for God to loose his soul."

Get away from him, May wants to warn, but there are others like him, so many others, she supposes, all over this city, gaunt in doorways, spitting up blood behind shutters. The man is convulsing now, howling, and May swallows hard, trying to keep down the nausea. The dread.

"The crowd follows the procession," Cristofana reports. "They're parading the fingernail of Saint Roch through the streets to ward away the Pest."

"What?"

"The priests have procured a relic of the saint—"

"Right," May says, fighting back bewildered tears, "a relic."

"The bishop and clergy advise that the procession should march through the city till nones," Cristofana continues matter-of-factly, her voice rising above the howling of the dying man. "There must be a hundred candles, as large as torches. Come look."

"No," May says, and starts walking again. "Thanks."

This street is familiar, and when the alley entrance appears, her heart starts racing.

It's clear from Cristofana's smug expression that she's been leading May here all along, to the artists' quarter.

It's all she can do not to run ahead and around the alley corner, but she lets her double keep the lead, and they pause under the entrance sign creaking on rusty chains in the wind.

Aching now to know that he's alive, May strides past Cristofana to peer through half-closed shutters. Relief hits so hard that she has to swivel away, sighing with her whole ghost body, melting into what she imagines is sun-warm stone, smiling at the ground. May knows the moment she looks up that she's given too much away, revealed a weakness, but it's too late.

A smile blooms on the other girl's face. "As I was saying, most shops have closed. But *some* are still here." Cristofana steps closer to the window, stroking the devoted kitten. "You think he's pretty, *bella*, don't you? I thought so, when I saw you together."

Gazing into the shadows of the workshop, where chickens peck at the dust, May grows hypnotized, watching as Cristofana watches, for the young man is alone inside, lost in dark thoughts, mourning someone perhaps—maybe his two friends, whose easels have been covered with dark cloth — staring fixedly at his drawing board.

May becomes so absorbed in his stillness that she doesn't notice Cristofana move. She doesn't see or sense the other girl's approach until her twin reaches around as if in embrace and tilts a coarse blade toward her neck, its tip extending between phantom May and the unshuttered window. "Do you remember this dagger?"

The knife doesn't rise, doesn't move but for the slightest tremble, but May shifts her focus from far to near, staring as if at a snake rising from its basket.

For a second, she holds her breath, waiting for Cristofana to run the blade across her tender neck with all her spite, do what those viper eyes promise (now that May's had the sense to turn around and face her), but what's worse than the look in her eye or the knife now vanished into her layers is the terror of what might lurk in her stolen clothing, of the microbes swarming, of death in the weave. Even in ghost form, with logic on her side (if her flesh and cells aren't active and present, then they can't be cut; they can't be infected), it's impossible not to panic.

May's done some reading since her last visit to Old Florence, and the Black Death — in an age without antibiotics — is about the scariest thing she can imagine.

The streets are more silent even than before, apart from the soft noise of the kitten on its haunches lapping from a bucket of filthy rainwater at the curb. Inside, the beautiful man stares, unmoving at his easel, but her gaze darts back to where the knife is concealed, in the contagion of her double.

"Relax, *bella*. You know by now that my knife cannot hurt you," Cristofana says, as if reading her thoughts. "You don't yet know or believe it, but you are the merest kind of visitor here, a traveler without footprints."

May looks in anxiously at the artist with the dark, sad eyes — alone, unaware of them outside his window.

"You worry for your flesh, but have you ever touched anything here, besides the ground you walk upon? Have you ever moved or altered anything or eaten a fig or"— she winks, gesturing —"stolen a kiss? You leave no mark, just as I leave none in your world. None is left on you."

May winces, remembering her knees, the blood, the strength and gentleness in the artist's hands, his smell. *You're wrong. I have.*

But what if Cristofana's right? What if passing through all ghostlike and leaving no mark is the real story of May's life — in Old Florence or New — in Vermont or Boston or anywhere else? Leave no mark and bear none. *He had touched her. He touched her and made her shimmer.*

"But we can change that," Cristofana offers, her voice hypnotic.

May shakes her head.

"Or do you imagine, as I sometimes do, that it was all just a very powerful dream — our trade before? Your meeting with Marco? For in dreams we have all we require."

May's eyes widen, and Cristofana continues cheerily, "Yes, I know him. I learned his name after you last left us. I made him notice me. Or helped him notice you? I should like very much to see your face when you cannot feel his lovely flesh as I can." She sighs as if the whole subject is profoundly tedious. "As I will. To distract from all this" — she waves an impatient hand — "death and sorrow.

"I have tried again, as flesh, to find your world. . . . I have labored without your selfish help. Sometimes, my fingers brush its edges. I hear its echoes. *Strega*, I say to myself, you have only to give back what you take. That is the rule. Until then you'll keep nothing. You don't believe me? In spite of all you've seen?" Balancing the kitten on one shoulder, she holds out her hand, and May recoils.

"Touch, Ghost."

"No."

"Are you afraid? Or you despise me?"

May lets her eyes answer for her.

"If not me, then him. Go inside to your precious Marco and take his hand. We can change fate by changing places, by fooling fate—"

May gapes at her, bewildered, and again at the lone figure inside the workshop. "That can't happen, Cristofana." To say the other girl's name is to humanize her somehow, make her real when she isn't. She—this—can't be real. "You know that."

"If I must stay, then I will do what I will. I will *have* my will."

May feels her pulse racing, desperation in every nerve. No, *but really, I want to give up modern medicine and hygiene, and the right to vote, and an education and career, and my family, and probably my life . . . to live . . . here . . . now . . . in filth and squalor and disease.* "Even if I could change places, I wouldn't," she says, staring in at him and fearing, even as she says it, that it's a lie. "There's a reason for all this."

"There is no reason," Cristofana snaps. "It is chance and my passion: I *will* you here. It's a rip in the air, a quirk in your fiber, and you deserve it less than I do." Cristofana stares at May and past her, stroking the kitten, with its wet whiskers and cloudy eyes.

Unnerved, May turns to the window again. She doesn't even pretend to hold back, just stares in at him, stricken, and wills him to look back. *It's me. See me. See me again.* She doesn't even know him, not really, but May can't persuade herself that it matters now. There's nothing here she understands except him, probably because he made her feel safe . . . in a place where nothing and no one is safe.

Every time he lifts the charcoal—and now that he has, he works feverishly, tilting his head, his shoulder rising and falling, his Adam's apple moving in his throat as he swallows—his black hair falls forward. He smooths it impatiently behind his ears, smudges the paper with his palm, his knuckles, and she feels his every gesture in her body as if her skin is breathing him, memorizing the way he moves, moving with him.

May has all but forgotten Cristofana, allowing herself to be careless around her for the last time. A cheery whistling calls her back, a little tune like a spell, and when May turns, transfixed, Cristofana is kneeling on the other side of the alley, smiling blackly. "You," she says, "are nothing here, *bella*, and you will listen when I speak to you."

Crouched beside the murky bucket by the door ledge, Cristofana holds the kitten under black water. It thrashes, its nails extended, raking the soft white flesh of her identical arm and drawing blood. Wet lines bloom on skin like marble shining in the Italian sun. The animal's head bobs out once with a yowling, but Cristofana pushes like a baker kneading dough, and though May tries, straining every muscle, she cannot move or change a thing. She cannot silence the voice chanting the word or reach out or call to the man indoors for help or stop the white arm dipping, the black water splashing, the little bedraggled body writhing, the air constricting. She can only gasp in the white-hot light, her face wet with tears.

"Nothing."

Iron in Her Blood

She is sobbing in the middle of a piazza, with strangers all around casting suspect glances. Pigeons bob and part under her feet as she hurries from alley to alley, finally slipping into the apartment. She retreats to her room and doesn't answer when Gwen knocks for dinner.

"I thought we could try Cafaggio again. What do you think? They had some OK veggie options."

"Give me a minute, Gwen," May manages to choke out. *A minute to find my mind. I've lost my mind.*

"Sure, love. We'll go grab a table. I could use a glass of wine. See you there?"

"Yes. OK."

"*Are* you?"

"What?"

"OK? You sound funny."

"I'm good," May murmurs. "Thanks."

When she hears their footfalls and the click of the ancient lock, she pads into the bathroom to splash cold water on her face. The bathroom mirror is still steamed from someone's shower, Liam's probably, since Gwen prefers baths, and May traces her own broad features — Cristofana's, she thinks, disgusted — on the wet glass, alarmed when her own red-rimmed eyes look back through the smear.

When she has it together enough to step out, she leaves the lower hall cautiously, afraid that the strange unreality of the crowded city streets might suddenly shift again and leave her lost, with or without a portal, send her back where the little animal floated in a bucket of black water. Focusing hard on the streetlights shining shadowy pink on stone and marble, on the busy murmuring of people heading out for the evening, she begins reciting the old rhyme "Step on a crack, break your mother's back," watching one foot move and then the other, and soon she's standing outside the restaurant, her chest taut with apprehension.

Gwen and Liam already have a table, so she threads

her way through the dinner line out front and lets the hostess lead her to them.

Liam doesn't look up when she sits down, so how can he see that she's on the edge of tears, that every move she makes feels tentative, wrong, as if her limbs don't belong to her, though she's somehow in charge of them? Maybe Gwen sees that something's wrong, but there's no way to tell with her, and her cheerful chatter doesn't hide the fact that Liam spends the better part of the night texting under the table, looking up only when the waiter brings his *arrosto misto*, a huge, steaming plate of every conceivable kind of meat.

About halfway through the meal, Gwen gets up to use the restroom. The second she rounds the corner, Liam reaches into his jacket for his phone, so May blurts out, as much for Gwen's sake as her own, "Quit acting like you have friends."

She says it jokingly: Liam has plenty of friends; he just isn't the type to chitchat on the phone with them or text back and forth all day, especially from a foreign country when it costs a fortune. He's avoiding her, and it's time she called him on it.

But she isn't prepared for how he responds—for the ice in his eyes and his ugly silence. When she stares him down, he finally blurts, "What's up with you, May? Maybe no one sent you the memo, but I was only thinking we could have a little fun while we're stuck over here together. Don't let it go to your head." He lifts a big chunk of lamb from his plate with his fingers and bites off a stringy corner, grease shining on his lips while he chews.

It's hurt talking, she knows; it's because she rejected him, but it doesn't make this any easier; it doesn't hurt her any less.

"You're always so sure of yourself and your tidy little world." He swallows, smiling like the Cheshire cat, taunting. "Well, you're not my type. You never were. I like a woman with a little meat on her bones, right? Some iron in her blood."

She concentrates on her dish of uneaten cabbage soup, oily and cold. May would explain if she could, erase what he's feeling, make up for it, but he's already paid her back in spades, and she's tired, determined not to cry. She doesn't owe him anything. What right does he have, expecting her to *have fun* and be available at his beck and call? Or did she lead Liam to think she wanted to? Is that where this went wrong? D*id* I? Do I?

"Got it, Li," May says, though she doesn't. She doesn't get anything anymore. "Loud and clear."

Standing, she lays her napkin over her bowl, hovering a moment, too embarrassed to let him watch her walk away. The white fabric soaks up broth, drooping into the dish. Li looks tired, too, almost sad now, staring past her.

She finally collects her bag and sweatshirt from the back of the chair, saying, "You think you know me, but you don't. You don't know shit."

He reaches for his phone again.

"Tell Gwen I went home with a stomachache."

Are You My Mother?

Wasn't she ever lonely before? May can't remember. She's never really understood loneliness. It's a word in songs — where people are so lonesome they can cry — especially the kind of folky songs her parents like, the kind that echoed from the radio on the cabin porch during summer vacations when they all sat watching dusk on the lake, when mayflies bumped against lanterns and nobody spoke, at least till the sun went down, because nobody had to. But in Maine, they were all feeling it together. They were wistful but content. That wasn't this.

It might be what her mother's been feeling, though. Maybe for years. Why had May never noticed? How could people walk around like this and no one notice? She's felt sad before, of course, hurt, pissed, but never *lonely*. It leaves you looking too hard into too many faces, too questioning, and strangers turn their eyes from you.

May feels hollow and sore inside and wants her mother in that big metaphorical way that the little bird in the old children's book wants his mother and goes around begging the dog, and the cow, and the steam shovel: "Are you my mother?" And they aren't. They never are . . . until . . . someone is. There's only one fit, one way to end that search, and finding that fit is the whole point, like finding a lock for a key you've carried around in your pocket your whole life.

Are you my mother? May thinks vaguely, watching people flow past, feeling stupid sitting here on a bench thinking about a thing she can't seem to do anything about. It isn't really her mother she wants; it's to not feel lonely anymore and for her mother to not feel lonely anymore. Why can't they *stop* each other from being lonely when they would do anything else for each other?

May imagines herself reflected in the darting eyes of passersby, an unhinged stranger in a strange land,

and suddenly she would do anything to not be here in a city, in a moment, when Gwen has to keep her nose buried in her notes because she doesn't know what to say (Gwen *always* knows what to say), when Liam is God knows where, pretending to e-mail his friends, when her own friends back home in Vermont, Sarah and Jenna, are sending messages like, *Guess who I saw today in the* Daily Grind*! Lol.* Her mother isn't calling or writing at all anymore, weary, no doubt, of the answering silence.

May gets up and begins to wander the crooked streets, trailing her hands over stone, imagining a door, a window, a rip in the air . . . a way in or out . . . a portal of her own. It's not that she wants to see Cristofana—what May *wants* is to wring her identical neck—but in some bizarre way, her freak twin and the skeletal face of plague, and the wolves and the *bechini* and the flagellants, the monks parading candles and saints' tongues through the streets, and Marco (*and Marco*) all feel more real to her than the good, ordinary people she's known and taken for granted her whole life long, people whose stories, like her own, are small but no less baffling for that.

I will you here . . . a quirk in your fiber.

She feels it again, that eerie presence from the bed-and-breakfast the first night she saw Cristofana, as if she's being watched. She can't find anything in her peripheral vision, but on the off chance that she is—that her twin is stalking her again—May speaks the words aloud, resolutely, like the crazy person she is, talking to herself on a bench: "I want to go back," she says, and if anyone hears, they just hurry past, "and see him again, alone. Open the portal from the alley outside his shop . . . into my room at the apartment. STAY AWAY . . . from it and from me. I'm thinking about your offer."

Back at the empty apartment, May pours a glass of milk. That noisy clock somewhere in the apartment, which she's never actually seen, ticks and ticks and ticks. She sits at the long butcher-block table under track lights and dunks a stick of almond biscotto into her milk, breaking it into softer and smaller bits. She looks around at Gwen's sprawl of books and papers, at Li's charging iPod, attached to his laptop, the apple glowing back at her like a forbidden fruit.

May wipes her milk mouth and drifts into her room. She changes her clothes, slips on leather sandals, and brushes her hair for a long, long time. Looking into her own eyes in the mirror, she can no longer trust them.

After a few moments, May senses it there, the portal, waiting. Open wide. She nonchalantly strides to the far rear corner of the room with her nerves screaming in revolt.

Testing with her hand, she steps through, struck as always by lightness, headache, and nausea. She thrusts out first one ghost arm and then the other, trailing her hand through stone as through water, letting dread and longing propel her into the street.

Her feet know the way—though she's trembling and everything echoes in an alarming way—and when she reaches the shop front, one shutter on the wide display window flaps open in a breeze, *thunking* the plaster wall.

May locates him at once in the gloom at the rear of the workshop.

He doesn't notice her out there in the hot white light, but when she ducks through the door, he looks up, astonished, and back at her with liquid, questioning eyes, eyes more hollow than before. He seems almost afraid.

It takes him awhile to stand, and when he does, he remains motionless for an unbearably long time, wrestling with what must be disbelief. When he finally reaches the door, gesturing her in with a few hoarse words of Italian May can't understand, he won't look at her at all, as if he doesn't trust himself . . . or her.

She tries to approach with the question in her eyes,

but he moves away, matching her step for step as if they're dancing. He closes his own eyes, rubbing the lids roughly with his palms, letting his hands fall to his sides again.

"What?" she asks softly, under her breath. "Did I do . . . something?"

The anguish in his face deepens. He can't understand her.

Either way, words are meaningless right now, and May isn't sure how to manage without them.

Marco's loose linen shirt or tunic is specked with paint, its sleeves rolled to the elbows. He smooths one down almost shyly, covering a sinewy forearm only to reveal wrinkled linen stained with what looks like egg yolk. He rolls the sleeve up again, apparently nervous, and when she tries to reach for his arm and assure him it's OK, that he shouldn't stand on ceremony for her sake, he flinches.

Shaking his head, he brings a slow forefinger to his lips, murmuring, "*I morti non parlano.*"

"Please," she tries, because she doesn't understand what he's saying—something about death, or the dead, and talking, speaking. *The dead do not speak.*

"Oh, no," she cries, shaking her head, "I'm not dead! I'm not a ghost. Please." But with every step she takes, he backs away.

She's reminded how tall he is, and his gravity and intensity embarrass her. May crosses her arms against the silence between them, and he smooths hanging hair behind his ears. It's a predicament, this communication thing, and in a way a blessing, since what is there to say? Where to begin?

Now he's eyeing her warily, his face drawn and sorrowful, and at long last he reaches for her, reaches through her, slowly, and lets his hand drop. He looks sick and astonished, deflated. When he turns away, it's with finality, crossing himself, as if May is just another figment of his artist's imagination or something worse. Something despised by God, which he must believe in, which everyone believed in then . . . now . . . even if the plague and its ravages have challenged those beliefs, as the history books claim.

She can only watch him go and trail soundlessly to the corner where he's taken his seat again. This time his easel is fitted with a tall wood panel—part of an altarpiece, she thinks. Gwen explained on some recent outing that altarpieces were commissioned, like a lot of religious art, as a way of telling Bible stories to the illiterate masses. The biggest churches had many, painted by leading artists of the day. Was Marco already a leading artist? Or had the plague smashed that social distinction, along with so many others? His master could already be dead, along with his fellows and competitors in the workshop — if the black cloths adorning their easels were any indication.

May stands as close as she dares, trying to breathe him in while he squints at the image emerging at the edge of the panel. He's decided she isn't here, that the plague has taken her like the others and she no longer exists as she did the day he bandaged her knee. The irony isn't lost on May: he who seemed to see inside her that day, to know her — body and soul — now refuses to see her at all. Can she blame him?

They will doubt their own eyes, Cristofana has said, *doubt their own minds*.

He stares trancelike at the unformed image on his board, and though she longs for him in a way that hurts, May finally accepts that she *isn't* here. Not like before. She couldn't touch him if she tried, not without Cristofana's permission, not without a "trade"— and forever is just too long. *But you are tempting*, she thinks, inhaling or imagining a rich blast of linseed oil or turpentine combined with the earthy smell of sweat, her fingers burning to trace his jawline. *Beyond tempting*.

He's pushed his hair out of his face and to one side, and May sees the sheen on the brown back of his straining neck and knows she wouldn't taste him either, if she bent down and touched her mouth to his skin the way she wants to.

As Marco cranes toward the forms emerging on the board, his body concentrating with his mind, all tension, May can only follow his movements with her eyes, touch and taste him in her thoughts, and she's almost glad he's given up on her shadow-presence, that his hollow, dark eyes are turned away. It would be like falling down a well, looking too long into those eyes, at least with this barrier, this layer of time or chance, between them. He might as well be a movie actor, a flat fantasy on a screen.

This is how true ghosts feel, May thinks, though she's never believed in ghosts before, and she begins to doubt—as he must—that he even saw her today.

You are nothing here.

With Cristofana's voice echoing in her thoughts, May turns toward the door, the street, the courtyard, the portal, letting the relief of now cover her like a wave.

Episodes

Since the portal conveniently leads home to her bedroom, May tries to take a nap, but she can no more rest her head than clear it. So she changes into shorts and a T-shirt and heads downstairs, walking in the general direction of the Uffizi. Somehow she knows she'll find Liam there. The museum not only has masterpieces in every room, Botticellis and Michelangelos and Raffaellos; it also has a room entirely devoted to Leonardo — the original Renaissance man and one of Li's heroes (more for his visionary scientific mind, perhaps, than his artistic one). They visited Saturday without Gwen, and it had to be the first time that May or anyone ever dragged Liam out the door of a museum and not the other way around.

Since then, he's already gone back once, and sure enough, May spots him today as she enters the far end of the walkway in the courtyard outside the gallery. He's resting on a low step in the sun, way down the pillared aisle by the niche with the statue of Galileo. Li has his headphones on and looks blank and more or less content with his own company, the late sun catching the red highlights in his hair. He might be waiting for her, May thinks — keeping out of view like the stalker she's apparently becoming, in one Florence or the other — but he isn't. May feels a sudden and terrible tenderness for him and almost strides across the loggia with the idea of grabbing those big bony hands fiddling with his iPhone and demanding, *Are you my mother?*

This cracks her up, and here's the funniest part: if she did do something stupid like that, say something that stupid and manage to explain herself before Li felt mocked and turned tail, he'd get it. They're *the same kind of stupid*.

Sensing something, he stirs uneasily on the step, checking the time on his phone. *What's for dinner? What am I waiting for?*

Me. May smiles. *You're waiting for me.*

When he gets up and heads out the entrance side of the almost deserted walkway, she follows from a distance, passing Dante in his niche, and all the other great men of Tuscany whose names she doesn't know, and finally, marble Galileo, his hand and bearded face raised toward the heavens.

Liam takes a long way back to the apartment, stopping in at Pegna—Gwen probably furnished a list—and when he emerges again with his brown bag, she trails him home, feeling good, better than she's felt in a long time, clearer.

When the front lock clicks, she presses her ear to the apartment door from outside. No voices. Gwen doesn't seem to be home yet. Good.

May wrestles her own key in the lock, breathes deep, and hurries to the kitchen before she can change her mind.

"Li?" she blurts, leaning in the doorway for support. "I'm sorry about the kiss."

He stares back at her, the expression morphing through hostility, defensiveness, amazement; he lays out his groceries on the counter. "You mean the non-kiss."

"Right," she admits, "but if we *did* kiss, it wouldn't be because we're going to hook up and be a thing—because we're not—but on the other hand, we trust each other, and I do want my first real kiss to be with you because there are too many things in this world you can't trust."

He takes his time, his brow drawn, emptying the brown paper bag, folding it carefully along the seam as she steps closer.

"Yeah," he says, deadpan. "Your first real kiss. I'm sympathetic with that, but no tongue. I draw the line at tongue. And don't think this means I trust *you*, because—"

She shuts him up, and it tastes good. He tastes good, and his mouth feels warm and hungry and comfortable, and she almost can't breathe and is ashamed to be thinking about Marco, thinking and kissing hard, which is wrong, very wrong. She knows that. When they pull apart, she wipes her mouth, almost reeling away, and tells him truly, "*Don't* trust me, Li. OK? I'm not trusting me right now."

Liam smirks, wiping his mouth, too, and shrugs a little wildly. "This is messed up, May—"

She catches his hand before he can walk away because she can't stand to lose him again. "It isn't you I wigged out about before. It's the end of *us* the way I knew us, easy. . . . When my parents told me this winter they were breaking up . . . I can't explain this to you—"

"Why not? You're forgetting my dad cut out pretty early."

May is struck. She hardly remembers Billy, Mr. Macintyre, but there he is suddenly, in her mind's eye, a smiling skinny man with a goatee and a mandolin and rockabilly sideburns. Two freckled arms, one with a mermaid tattoo, throwing them off the dock into the icy Maine water. That feeling she had remembered on the porch earlier today, with the dusky lake and the mayflies and the wistful content, that was Billy and his mandolin, not the radio. He'd been a part of that feeling, and she had forgotten him.

Liam's waiting eyes are so good right now, and his chapped lips, and those hesitant hands that just a minute ago were moving in her hair. She wants to kiss him some more, wants to feel him press her back against the fridge, wants to stop longing for what she can't have, or at least share the unfamiliar crush of longing; she wants to just relax, but she can't. And she won't use him that way, even if he wants her to. But she can't let him retreat back into that funk, either. "Can I tell you something?" May leads him by the hand over to a stool at the breakfast nook, where he sits obediently. She has to twist her hand free and back away before she can concentrate on her words. "Something weird?"

"Always." He studies her with more patience than she deserves. "Look who I was raised by. 'Weird' is my birthright."

"Well, I'm having these . . . episodes."

"What kind?"

"Time . . . episodes."

He nods slowly. "All right, I'm with you so far."

"Where I'm here, and then I'm . . . there."

" 'There' being what? West Virginia? Topeka?"

"Here. Florence. But back in 1348 or so . . . around the time of the plague. There's this girl who looks like me, and she's sort of twisted."

"That I believe." He shrugs when he sees that she isn't kidding. "You're messing with me, right? To get my mind off the fact that you're willing to kiss me when you don't really want to?"

"I want to, Li. Just not as much as you want me to."

"What else are you willing to consider wanting less than I do?"

She sighs, and he sighs back.

"I wish I could explain . . . all of it. But I don't understand myself. . . ."

"OK. So there's this girl in 1348. Maybe she'll be into me." He shrugs, smiling wanly.

"You have no idea how much that disturbs me."

Do you think he's pretty, bella?

"Then you're jealous?"

"She's not very . . . nice."

"So she's, like, some kind of mean, dangerous version of you? Even better. Maybe you can learn from this girl, dude."

"Li. I'm serious. Something's wrong with my head. This trippy thing . . . keeps happening."

He frowns to get his face in order. "Well, what's it like? Describe it. Maybe we'll find something online."

She nods gratefully—hadn't dared go online before, alone; it made it too real—and they put their heads together in the Google glow of his laptop.

"You really are your mother's son, you know." May smooths the fox-brown hair from his eyes so he can see the screen. "It's all about the research."

Liam slaps her hand away lightly. "If you want my help, leave my dignity intact, OK?"

"'Kay."

"But will you kiss me again if I find out something?" He leans sideways, just slightly, typing in keywords. "Because you smell good."

"I'll think about it."

The Safety of Where You Stand

Cristofana leaves the portal open in May's bedroom to tease her, no doubt, and the new reckless May, the one willing to play Russian roulette with her life, actually does sneak through that week, twice, but only for as long as it takes to get to the workshop and back.

She does it to catch a hungry glimpse of him, assure herself the artist is still there, still alive—but she also does it to remind herself that the impossible is possible.

May lives in abject terror the entire time she's on the other side, her nerves screaming because it would be easy, should Cristofana spot her floating along the cobbled, dead-strewn streets of Old Florence, for her twin to seize the opportunity and slip through to the present, closing the door with May stranded in the distant, terrible past.

But May is gambling, in part, on Cristofana's short attention span. (How long could her twin, however determined, realistically lurk around the portal entrance? She had to eat, forage, survive.)

Out May steps into the glare of yesteryear in her same drab dress and sandals, dodging the living and the dead in her haste. She knows the way by heart now, and she's sworn to herself that she won't upset him in ghost form again, so her visits are brief but heady. He can't see her out there, even if he glances up from his corner toward the window ledge. (May often wonders why he chooses to work back there in the shadows; aren't artists always after the "good light"? Not Marco, apparently.) She's invisible in the relentless Italian sun. Present—and unbearably absent.

But one day Cristofana does catch May out. She's loitering beside the portal when May emerges, and she sidles up before May can backtrack.

"There is only one way to be with him, you know." She follows May out of the hushed alley, into the cobbled streets. "You know this, don't you?"

May decides to play along. "If you want me to stay today," she snaps, "don't leave my sight. If you do, I'll assume you're out to trap me. If I stay, it's on my terms."

Cristofana smiles indulgently, bending at the knee as for royalty. "As you wish."

They both know that all Cristofana has to do is get back to the portal before her and slip through, but May's counting on whatever it is that's been holding Cristofana back this long.

There has to be something.

It's early, and the streets are hot and dry, deserted but for the occasional vagrant with downcast eyes. The sun beats down like a bludgeon. So May makes little effort to conceal her ghost self.

They pause at the end of an alleyway to let a carriage pass so it doesn't mow Cristofana over, and the girl slouches against a wall in her weird array of rags and pilfered riches. May looks up, really, for the first time — at least on this side of time — and is shocked to find no dome. Il Duomo, the focal point of the city she knows, isn't here. May's never bothered to lift her head (or dared take her eyes off Cristofana for long), but apparently the first marvel of modern architecture, as Gwen called it the day they arrived in Florence, hasn't been built yet. May's uneasy gaze darts left and right, seeking the gold doors Gwen showed her. They aren't here, either. Together with the general air of horror and decay in the city, the pestilence has halted all construction. There's a chaotic, unfinished air about everything.

The carriage is stuck in a pothole, the driver whipping the horse while a passenger leans his weight against the wheel, and Cristofana stops to watch. May sees that the scratches on her wrist are still there, fainter but an ugly pink, infected probably.

"How could you?" May accuses now, remembering, most of all, her own helplessness.

"How could I *what?*" The other girl blinks back disdain.

"Do what you did to that animal. It trusted you."

Recognition blooms on her mirror face. "Kitty, kitty, poor kitty—"

If May were flesh and blood, her fingernails would be biting into her palms. Cristofana surprises her then by stepping forward, standing as close as she can get without blurring with May. "That cat was skin and bones, riddled with worms, with none to care for it." Her voice is low and dire, and May hates the truth in her words. In May's future, kittens are routinely dewormed; it's a common treatment, one she herself helped administer over and over during a veterinary internship the summer after sophomore year. The bony gray kitten had lived in a state of constant, nagging hunger, a hunger no food would solve, *which is no excuse for murdering it*, May thinks, but then again, there seems to her no excuse, no possible explanation, for tearing your holy men limb from limb, either.

"You live in an easy world, yes?" Cristofana complains, as if reading her mind.

Yes, May thinks, I *do, but it's all relative.* Everything's *relative.*

"You are full of goodness and generosity, but have you learned nothing here?" Cristofana turns like a dancer, her frayed silks twirling. "Come, let me walk you to the parish churchyard, where they've dug trenches down to the waterline, wide and deep. Every night, people of good conscience, or those paid handsomely for their trouble, haul the dead on their backs and hurl them into this hole without ceremony. Every morning, the bodies are sprinkled over with earth. Come night again, more are heaved on top . . . crisscross double-cross, as the good rhyme goes . . . and then more dirt, and so on, layered like a mamma's lasagna. Gone are the processions and blazing candles, the pretty cloaks and mantels and veils for the lady mourners, the bells and biers and wailing multitudes. Instead, you vanish. You are plowed under and forgotten. Like that." She snaps her fingers, gazing at them almost proudly, and then walks on.

May lets her go.

"Well?" the other calls back haughtily, pausing again. "Will you not face what I do daily? Will you judge me from the safety of where you stand?"

"I've seen enough."

"Have you?"

"There's nothing I can do to help. It's all happened. It's over—"

"For *you* it's over. Do you not see that our world is gone mad with the pestilence? We are no more good and evil. In this suffering and misery of our city, the authority of human and divine laws is no more. The ministers are dead or sick or shut up with their families. None do their duty, and to spite them, we do as we please, and who can blame us when we will die anyway, good or bad? God wills it, and He is cruel."

Two huddled women in fine dress hurry past. If they *don't* see May or don't believe what they see, it's a fierce lone girl in strange clothes they perceive, a stupefied madwoman ranting on a street corner. If May is visible—and who knows?—it's all a trick of the light, and the women lower their eyes so quickly that they see two eerily identical girls, one flesh and one phantom, arguing. Either is cause to cross the cobbles, crushing sprays of herbs and posies under their nostrils. The air here reeks of death and sickness, so those who can afford to carry nosegays or vinegar-soaked rags to ward away the stink.

May stares back, unyielding, her lip trembling.

"If you will not look around you, will not take what I offer, then give *me* something. I love this city, loved . . ." A glimmer of sorrow, rare and compelling on the mirror of May's own features, is all it takes.

May feels her anger recede, eclipsed by pity.

"Give it back to me, my city."

"What do you want me to say? There's no end to it, if that's what you mean—sickness, war, violence—it doesn't go away. It gets worse. There are machines in my world, so many machines, and everything's faster."

"But what of Firenze?"

"In just a few decades," May explains, straining to orient herself in time, to access Gwen's or Liam's latest lecture on the Renaissance, "Florence will be one of the most celebrated cities in the world. There's a rebirth of ideas here . . . and all these great painters and musicians and architects. There'll be a huge dome . . . up there . . . and gigantic gold doors, there and there."

"These I have seen with my own eyes. You forget . . . I am a traveler, too. But go on. It's true, then, as Marco says, that men will one day care for more than sheep and wool and commerce?"

For a moment, May doesn't register the name, and when she does, she feels a violent stab of jealousy. So they've talked? In their native Tuscan dialect, no doubt. "Yes," she says, her tone cold, firmer, "and medicine. People won't get sick so often or die from sickness, at least not in developed countries."

"Developed?" She looks puzzled. "I knew you were not from Firenze, but from where? You learned your speech in England? I learned it from my English mother."

"My country doesn't exist yet. Or at least not the way it does later. Medicine could ease this sickness, but there'll be another. Just as there are other wars. Nothing is easy. No time is easy. In the country where I live, two vast buildings, taller than twenty of your city towers, were blown from the world with all the people in them. You have a choice."

"A choice?"

"How you endure it."

"*You* have a choice. I must make do with your word, it seems. You speak of history, not life. But continue."

May thinks of the newscasts, the photographs, the smiling portraits of those killed in the attacks of 9/11. She was just a kid and mostly remembers her mom's silence. Her dad's tears. "No. I'll give you nothing until you . . . apologize . . . for what you did to that cat, for who you are."

"Then I make my choice." Cristofana turns and sets off marching.

"Where are you going?" May demands, wrestling with foreboding, her voice shrill.

"With luck, I'll *choose* to kill a nun," Cristofana calls over her shoulder, an obscene smile on her face as she strides through the maze of streets and alleys with May at her heels. "I'll slit her throat with my knife. Now, *that* will be a choice."

As they cross into the artists' quarter, May feels a terrible, reeling sense of dread, a now-familiar sensation where Cristofana's concerned.

"And you must understand that no one will miss her. No one misses anyone now. We disappear, and no one sees. Can you begin to know this feeling, *bella?*"

The city shops and guilds have all been officially closed, Cristofana explained earlier, to contain infection, but every so often as May follows on this fool's errand, she sees individual merchants and craftsmen enter or exit buildings, and now and then she makes out the dim glow of torches or candles between shutters. When they reach the familiar street-level *bottega*, she pants, "Stop . . . please."

Cristofana does and turns. "Oh, don't look at me with those child's eyes."

"Your eyes," May challenges.

"No, *bella*. Mine have seen more. Much more."

May turns in frustration, running her palm along the wall, or trying, imagining the coarse drag of the brick she can't feel. Her skin and bones and beating heart all scream to be here and impact things, to have power in this place, but they don't.

"Oh, you are so good, aren't you? You despise cruelty. You are like a good little nun. You are no use to him at all."

Him. That pronoun again.

They have reached the workshop, and Cristofana peers around the loose shutter, spying.

May sidles up next to her, eager and afraid at once. She wants to see him again, badly, as always, and there's a kind of shame in that. It clouds her judgment, and Cristofana knows it. She's the *only* one who knows. May feels complicit in something, and this helpless craving for something to happen, for relief, is agonizing. "How can you stand to be you?" May hisses near the other girl's ear.

But together they admire his lean back in a soiled linen shirt, the thoughtful tilt of the black back of his head, the geometry of his raised arm. There is color everywhere, streaking his clothes, the stiff chair and those beautiful hands, speckling the plank floor. The workshop is a sweaty, close space, full of wooden bowls of ground pigment and sticky paint, hunks of half-chiseled stone, piles of charcoal-marked pages, sheets of hammered bronze, dust falling through beams of light, the ubiquitous chickens picking through curls of wood for a dropped almond. Squat candles burn on an iron stand. "The same way I can do this. Watch, now. His light is burning for me."

She has her hand on the door latch before May can blink, and suddenly Cristofana's inside. It's as if a real person has walked onto a television set, into the screen. He doesn't flinch when she comes slinking up from behind. She lifts a leg and swivels, sliding between the artist and his easel, settling on his lap, facing him, and for a moment he looks around the empty workshop, stunned and bewildered, but he soon relents hungrily, hands moving over her neck and breasts. She kisses him hard, grinding on his lap, and May turns away in an agony of disgust. Is he kissing Cristofana because she's there, because he can, the way May imagines she kissed Liam? *Does he think it's me? Doesn't he know it isn't? Why should he care? He thought I was dead. . . .*

Her rage doesn't make it any easier to look away from the spectacle in front of her, her artist's strong, scarred hands roving over Cristofana's face, in her hair. *Mine,* May thinks—and this childish greed is new and terrible—*mine.*

Cristofana breaks the seal of their kiss, arching her back, glancing up at the window for effect, wiping her smug mouth. The two exchange a few words May can't hear, their foreheads touching, his mouth brushing her neck. Almost as quickly as she slipped away, Cristofana returns, adjusting her clothes. May stands speechless by her mirror image until it presumes to speak in that low, dire voice May hates, the one that purrs like a secret. "He will die, you know. More important, I will die, unless you save me. *Save me*, and take him for your trouble."

Their eyes lock.

"Oh, his hands feel good, *bella*. I must tell you. He is an apprentice only, but a master with his hands, and he tastes like honey from the hills. His mouth is warm, and twice already he has painted me nude."

"Shut up, you"—it slips out before May can stop it, a word she doesn't use, just wouldn't ordinarily use, but this anger is so rich, so comforting—"*bitch*."

"Now then, my friend, what harm in it? In being a little dog, a little she-dog, licking his—?"

"*Shut* up!"

"He saw you then, but now he sees only me. He thinks I am you, and I will treat him unkindly in your name. I will seduce him and break his heart. I will ruin his good, damaged soul and take his smile forever in your honor, and he will think all along it was you, the girl who came from another world and loved him with her eyes.

"You should not go away so long, *bella*. You never know what will happen, and you care too little for him. You care too little for me when you might help me. You have but one choice and that is to *make* a choice.

"Stay here. Take your chances with Marco. The pestilence will pass, and he will be a great artist like his master, one of your Renaissance men — with all the best patrons one day, all the best commissions — and you will wear silk like my lady did, before she died in a puddle of filth, before the buboes came.

"Stay, and I will go, and we will cheat time, which will not otherwise let us each have what we want."

"I don't know what I want," May admits, hating herself for it, and somewhere in the back of her head, she hears her mom's voice intruding, calm and measured — on the day she and Dad broke the news — her own mother's voice, saying, "There is no logic in love, no knowing when it will come . . . or go." Even her father seemed to hold with this ridiculous statement, murmuring agreement, nodding meekly.

Is this love?

How tame May has been all her life, how trusting

and well behaved and unimaginative. Always doing the right, expected thing. *I am not myself*. Even her parents are braver, and May feels the injustice of this like a red blaze, a fury she turns on her double. "Not that your plan is in any way, shape, or form *sane*. Has it ever occurred to you that I like my life?"

"Has it ever occurred to *you*? I have watched you—when you didn't know I was there—sitting glumly with your loved ones, picking at your food (so much food!). You have everything. You deserve none of it."

They stare at each other until Cristofana resumes in her headlong way. "But I digress. Only think: you and Marco will have babies, and you will keep kittens, fat kittens—you'll be a hero to kittens—and I will have—"

What? May thinks, smelling or imagining the hint of sickness and decay in the air, the chill damp in the stones, easily eclipsed in her mind by the warmth of his hands, his hot eyes on her. *I am not myself*. She shakes her head, shakes herself sensible. "I'm going home to think. But first tell me—you're obviously dying to—what *you'll* have. What's in it for you . . . after you've saved your sorry ass?"

"What do you suppose?" May's twin blinks back at her, the soul of patience. "I will have everything that is yours, *bella*." She glances over May's shoulder. "Now, go from me. I have an unpleasant errand."

May glares at her. Cristofana is a schemer, a survivor, and it makes sense that assuming May's identity would offer safe haven in an alien world. It would buy her time to orient herself. *The more she knows about my life, the more prepared she'll be to take it over.* "Tell me how the portal works," May demands, remembering that she has questions of her own. "How are you doing this?"

"The spells are here. And here." Cristofana touches her palm to her forehead, her chest. "They can't be told or sold or borrowed." She walks away, calling over her shoulder. "Make the choice with your heart, *bella*, not fear, and make it soon. I grow weary, waiting."

Another Day

May watches her double walk away, the long tangle of dirty-blond hair laced through with tiny dreadlock braids, ribbons, and straw, her scavenged gown-of-the-day, a busty plum number, dragging in the muck. Watching her grow smaller on the horizon, a purplish speck, May panics. Letting Cristofana out of her sight here is like losing sight of herself somehow, and when the other girl veers down a crooked alleyway, May starts after her, a ghost streaking the air.

May follows through a stony labyrinth of streets, keeping well out of view, and then across a busy covered bridge. She guesses it's an earlier incarnation (this version looks almost newly constructed) of Ponte Vecchio, but instead of the rows of flags and *trattorias* and stalls offering souvenirs and fancy jewelry, there are tables manned by burly butchers and tradesmen advertising their wares. Luckily there's enough streaming light inside to conceal her as she dodges in and out of the shifting crowd.

Through the archways, May sees the river below, wide and flat and shining, dotted with tiny men rowing tiny boats (though May knows that up close they're probably the long *barchettas* still used, in the future, to give river tours).

When Cristofana steps onto the Arno's other bank, though, May hesitates. There isn't a cloud in the perfect blue sky today, but it's hard to believe you're invisible—when you aren't used to being—so as she comes into the open, May has to make it unaccosted past one or two bridge-bound travelers before she can relax. When no one notices her on the winding cart road through green and gold hills dotted with cypress and silvery olive trees, she breathes easier, keeping her plum-colored target in view.

At last Cristofana turns down a scrubby dirt pathway with grass and blue chicory growing around the wheel tracks, startling a wild rabbit or hare out of hiding. She stops at what appears to be a church, if the crude wooden cross out front is any clue, or perhaps a convent. It's a shabby building with a garden and a small stable off to one side, though there's something familiar about the layout of the buildings or the angle of the view, and it hits May that the trek she just made follows the same route — through a much-changed, or at least more populated, landscape — that she and Gwen and Liam took down from that bed-and-breakfast in the hills the day they first arrived in Florence City Center. The only difference was that their cab had crossed one of the handful of other city bridges. Future Ponte Vecchio was open only to foot traffic.

Was this the original "medieval nunnery" mentioned in the B&B's brochure?

Her double lurks out front for a long time, pacing back and forth as if trying to make up her mind. The sound of bells nearby seems to trigger a decision, and rather than lift the iron knocker, she slips around the long, low stone building and cautiously approaches a small fenced kitchen garden in back. Here, three women wearing black veils and dresses of rough brown cloth kneel in the soil, weeding.

Cristofana stands stock-still by the figure nearest

the gate, her shadow falling over a woman with hollow eyes and hair pulled back severely under her veil. She looks to be about ten years older than Cristofana but is possibly younger, May thinks, and worn down by what must be a difficult life of labor and sacrifice.

May floats closer to get within earshot, holding her breath, feeling exposed, though she isn't.

It takes the woman a long while to look up, as if she's delaying on purpose, but the minute she lifts her face, May sees the resemblance. The woman stands, wiping earth-black hands on her sack dress, and under her steady gaze, Cristofana averts her eyes. The two kneeling nuns now stand, too, nodding or bowing as they pass Cristofana, filing out of the fenced-in garden in silence. They disappear inside the convent.

"Marietta," Cristofana says crisply. Her gaze is still turned to the ground, from what May can tell, and her knotted hands fidget behind her back. What she's really doing, May sees, is slipping that honking red ruby off her finger. The ring vanishes into her basket. "I mean, Suor Arcangela, of course."

"Of course you do." The woman regards the girl, who must look garish to her, in her plum-colored dress and ratty ribbons. With a curt nod, Marietta, or Sister

Arcangela, walks the length of the fence, her own hands stiff behind her back. "Cristofana." Her face is hard to read. "You have traveled long?"

"You are well," the other asks with a contemptuous wave, "here?"

"I am always well." The nun never turns her grave eyes from the other's dress. "I need for little . . . here."

"Yes, yes, I know," Cristofana complains, her voice rising. "I read your letters. With your vow of poverty, you sleep in the straw on the hard ground. You wake in the night for Matins. You pad barefoot to meet your bridegroom Christ by candlelight. You are a slave, and it shows in every line on your face."

The nun's face flushes red. "And you are an aberration." She breathes deeply, composing herself. "God, who is Master of all, forgives you, sister, as do my thirty true sisters. As do I," she adds, almost kindly, though the edge in her voice is obvious. "It's been some time since I wrote to our mother, who for too long didn't answer. You look ridiculous," she blurts out, a distracted smile ghosting on her lips, "of course, as always—a preening doll. Like her."

Cristofana drops into a curtsy. "There is reason enough Mamma stopped writing, but where to begin. You do not refuse to speak her language, I see."

"It is not her language I object to . . . or her nation

of origin. Our mother may be vain and foolish, but she turns a pretty phrase, and I welcome the chance to practice the English tongue. My studies occupy me much. Even now. Even . . . here," the woman adds, parroting her younger sister's tone. Her face changes — softens. "You have the news, then, you and Mamma?"

Cristofana turns away, shading her eyes against the glare, bracing herself, probably.

"Babbo is dead."

There's nothing in her expression to suggest that this news upsets her. No surprise. No change in her posture. But by now, May knows Cristofana well. Something has collapsed in her. Broken.

"Taken by the Scourge at sea," continues Suor Arcangela, who was once plain old Marietta, somebody's big sister. Cristofana isn't quite an orphan, after all. "So many long years at sea, and this as his homecoming. Ludovico, his loyal servant, survived — one of the few aboard who did — and delivered Sire's diary. He could not find Mother to notify her, and later I will ask you why not."

Cristofana waits intently, hands limp at her sides. May has never seen her so mute and still.

"He died in the dark of night — or so in my solitude I imagine, for here his book turns silent, its pages mute — huddled in his own arms in a corner of a sloshing galley ship." Sister Arcangela speaks in a low, lilting voice, like someone entranced. "Their galley put in at Genoa in January, driven by a fierce wind from the East. Sire wrote of how spices and silks from the East reached the markets of Europe via Baghdad. They moved along the Tigris through Armenia to the stations of our merchants in the Crimea. It was no wonder, he observed, that the pestilence — some said it cloaked itself in a poison cloud, a very corruption of the air, a miasma born of the filth of toads, lizards, and rats — should take these trade routes, too. That the great caravans would spread disease first among the Tartars and then the Genoese. Night and day, he wrote, while fearless rats sniffed from their holes to lap at vomit and waste and were kicked dead against the walls, men whispered it. The ship was cursed. The Pest was a punishment from God, they said, against those who make hay with the Turks and Saracens who raze Christian cities."

"Did Babbo raze cities?" Cristofana accuses, her voice shrill. "No . . . like those others crowded aboard a curse, he rocked and retched and was baffled and terrified of God. Your precious God."

"If you do not walk here with Him, sister, then walk away." Suor Arcangela motions toward the silent, hulking convent. "The orphans behind those walls, their numbers growing every day, still court His grace. You would deny them?"

Cristofana paces the fence line, her pale hand tracing splintered wood. "I will walk, Marietta, and do not for a moment suppose I'll look back. . . . I came only to say good-bye."

"If you go, take care. This disease spreads so quickly. . . . It seemed to our father that the end of the world must be near, for the horror no one spoke aloud on that ship was that people, other people, are the biggest threat of all. Death travels in the kindly stroke of a forehead, in a kiss or a sigh, in the fingernails of a pained man digging into his wife's wrist. You have heard the same rumors in Firenze? That pigs snuffle human garments only to topple down dead? It lurks in a lover's breath or a mother's lullaby, and in Christian courage—for the monks and priests die by the day, and our own ranks here, before we know to cross ourselves. Worst of all, it lives in a look, a look alone.

"Babbo, before he died, blamed the dour old man in the corner, the first aboard to sicken and die, who had fixed him with that blank stare that promises, *Here I am, and here, too, you will be.*

"Our father was tossed unceremoniously overboard like the others, so many others, food for sharks. Though the ship's belly was bloated with silks and spices, riches beyond measure, every belly on that vessel was empty. The food ran out, and the living were turned away from port after port, the galley driven away by flaming arrows and diverse engines of war. For no man would touch them. Ludovico and three fellows stole away at night in a rowboat.

"You need not go," she segues almost gently. "Mother Abbess and the sisters would welcome your help and give you refuge. It is a dangerous time."

"So that I might live for broth and pealing bells? For Matins and Lauds and Terce? So that I might speak of nothing but alms and intercessions and touch my forehead to the cold stone? Never."

"Never is a long time."

"Never is never."

"You are stubborn, Cristofana, and young."

"You are stubborn and old."

"Come back, then, and tell me your news. Bring some bread for the children. Another day."

"Another day."

May is shocked, when Cristofana turns in profile, to see her twin's dirty cheeks streaked with tears. She swipes them away fiercely, frozen to the spot like startled prey. Swiping again, Cristofana strides away, and May knows she'll have to overtake her on (or off) the road, beat her twin back to the city and the alley and hustle through the portal, but for an instant she's too stunned to move.

Sister Arcangela watches her sister go with sorrowing eyes, making the sign of the cross over her heart.

Sleepwalking

May knows she is dreaming, for real this time, safe in bed.

She wakes, in the dream, under a rough blanket, tangled in a crimson gown, her chest tight with dread. A baby is crying, somewhere, and the sound holds the night like an egg in its palm. It rakes the brain like blades, and there are no slamming doors or searching voices. No reassuring sirens. No noise of rescue. Only a lone, intermittent cry of pain and outrage that echoes everywhere.

May has no idea how or when the cries sounding from all sides and none began to saw at her sleeping thoughts.

Gone are the soft cotton bedclothes, the scalloped plaster walls, the hemp robe and plush towel hanging on the door hooks, the switch for the overhead light. Her hand gropes stone as she pads through hollow rooms she recognizes by their contours only. She makes her way to a shutter flapping in a damp wind. Slumped over the terrace ledge, she looks out over the sparkling river and the torch-lit bridges punctuating it at intervals, at a bright half-moon.

Wherever it is, the child is hungry, wet, possibly sick. The sound seems to come from everywhere at once but mainly from behind the building, in the tangle of crooked streets far below. May's nerves scream with panic. How can you help someone you can't find?

Coming, she pleads in mind. *I'm coming. Please stop crying.*

Feeling her way in the dark through the front room to the door, May knows she has to get outdoors and find this small, needful thing whose hiccupping cries have grown jagged and pitiful.

May.

She is running in bare feet over sharp, damp cobbles, running blindly. They collide when she turns into the alley in the artists' quarter, and May feels an animal rush as sinewy arms close round and contain her. Crushed against his chest, she feels fear and safety, heat and sorrow, and when she looks up, falling into the well of those eyes — a well echoing with promises in another language — he takes her breath in a deep kiss.

The wailing child stills, and it's a long, sweet silence, but beyond the city walls of Old Florence, a collective howl builds slowly, brimming like a too-full glass, and in reply, one baby becomes many, a shrieking cacophony.

May.

"Hey," Gwen urges softly, her eyes startled and concerned in the halo of lamplight around her reading chair. "Wake up. You're sleepwalking again."

"Again?" May blinks, confused. *They roam like the ravenous wolves that circle the city walls at night, smelling death.*

"Second time this week. Liam found you last time on his way to the bathroom. You were headed for the terrace. Um, he was supposed to talk to you about it."

May sits down at Gwen's feet and lays her head against the older woman's bony knees with a sigh. "I'm sorry."

Gwen strokes her hair from behind, leaning in.

"Look, kiddo. I know you don't want to"—she tries to lift May's stubborn chin—"but maybe we need to call Ann. Maybe we should call your parents."

May shakes her head violently. "You're right. I don't want to."

"Really? Or you're just being a martyr?"

"Really." May looks up quickly. "Listen, we will. I will, but not now. I'm just thinking it through."

"It?"

May wonders what, if anything, Liam has told Gwen about May's behavior—his theories about it, anyway. She's tempted in that moment of comfort to spill everything, all of it, relent and let them get her a counselor, get her some meds, get her better, get her over it. *Him*. Over fear and fascination and lust and rapture.

But some instinct prevents her. "I just need a cup of tea," she says coyly, looking away, and Gwen brightens, setting her book aside on the coffee table.

In May's experience, grown women, especially insomniacs, can't resist the healing properties of tea.

Hallucinating in Detail

Distracted at dinner the next night, May tries to smile when Gwen pokes her with the handle of her spoon.

"I'm glad to see you two are back on track. I was beginning to get worried." Mother and son have been grappling over tiramisu at Caffagio, and Gwen's contemplating the last spoonful, turning it this way and that. "Now I'm worried I ought to be worried about something else instead."

May and Liam both glare at her. "Didn't your mother ever counsel you not to talk with your mouth full?" May complains.

Gwen goes on smiling with her eyes in a really infuriating way. "Madlenka's treating me to a night out, remember? I trust you two have plans?"

Liam rolls his eyes. "Yes, Ma, we do, or I do, and I figured May might tag along, not that we're joined at the hip or anything—"

"What else would I do?" May interrupts, leaning forward on her elbows. "Do what?"

Gwen dabs at the edges of her mouth with her napkin to hide her smile. She's way too happy about this "worry" of hers, which tempts May to rebel against the whole prospect in advance.

She picks at her dessert and lets her mind drift to Marco for spite. She hasn't been through the portal in days, partly because of a succession of dream/sleepwalking incidents like last night's. It just feels too risky, with the dates matching up the way they do. The plague is in full force. May can only imagine what's happening back there, and it terrifies her.

Tonight, everything's blurry and blended. Plague or no plague, she feels fat and full and reasonably content, or at least grateful to be alive, which is saying a lot—but is she watching Liam's mouth this way because she can't watch Marco's? Is she that fickle? Does Li mean that little to her? Or that *much*? And which is it?

Liam doesn't seem to want any part of Gwen's

smirking, either. He answers her question in a bored voice, his eyes trained on some invisible point across the room. "This Austin band's playing downtown. They're here on a European tour, real hick-downer, shoegazer shit." He pauses a second, looking at Gwen, but she doesn't object — she's in a good mood, evidently, having paired off her two favorite young people and moved on with her stimulating life post-parenthood. *Her and everyone else*, May thinks, petulant.

"The guy has a voice somewhere between honey and rust," Liam's saying, and May wonders if he gets this kind of talk from his father. She always forgets that their family is musical. For a lot of years, before the court-appointed visits ended, Mr. Macintyre (though he wouldn't let anyone call him that; he was always "Billy") gave Liam guitar lessons. They even wrote a couple of songs together. "It'll make you want to drink yourself to death," Liam says, "which is my kind of fun. And they have a great fiddle player."

Gwen offers May a pitying smile but doesn't comment on the booze concept, so Liam hurries on. "I know it's cheating" — he sighs — "and that we should go find dudes doing accordion or opera or the strobe-trance European thing or something, but I'm homesick. There. I said it."

"Sounds fun," May says sincerely, dropping her

spoon into her empty dish with a groan just before the waiter swoops it up, eager to turn his table, no doubt. She means it, and Liam settles back, his persuasive work done. He plows the salt and pepper shakers to the edge of the table with his forearm, rolls Gwen's receipt into a compact puck, and bats it over with his fork. "Hockey?"

"Geez," May says, fishing the receipt out of her lap and batting it back with her butter knife. "You *are* homesick."

Gwen heads to the restroom, and the game continues in that soothing, halfhearted way such games do. May, meanwhile, considers how going out to see some band from Texas in a bar in Florence is a reasonably ordinary "young adult" thing to do if you happen to *be* in Florence. As it turns out, she has next to no experience being an ordinary nocturnal high-school student. Home in Vermont, she almost never went out, even on weekends. Unless her school friends rallied hard, she didn't feel the need. May was content at home, unlike most kids her age. Home with her parents and True—each of whom was quiet in the same essential way and respectful of the others' quiet—was enough. But that home didn't exist anymore. At the moment, it had to be a gaping shell, with all Mom's stuff trucked off to Boston and Dad's in a funk of neglect. What would her mom's new place look like? Would Dad hire a housekeeper?

A week ago, these questions would have nagged at her in the worst way, the choice they're forcing her to make would have wrenched her insides, but Liam's invitation (if you can call it that) reminds her that there's a world out there. There'll be college in that world and concerts and maybe boyfriends. A *boyfriend*, May thinks, glancing up at Liam involuntarily when Gwen leaves for the coatroom and thinking at the same time that *boyfriend* is a stupid word, childish—how do you cram the big bad rush she feels for Marco into a word like that? The artist seems to have woken something up in her that was sleeping, something she didn't know was there, and even if he won't be in her world, can't be in it, this brave new tomorrow of hers seems poised and electric, full of possibility.

"Why didn't you bring your guitar this trip?" she asks.

"Haven't played in a while."

"You miss it?"

"There's always something to miss." Liam flicks the puck past her again. "That's game." He brushes her wrist with two fingers, so quickly she might have wondered afterward if it even happened—except for the goose bumps. "I'll miss you. When summer's over."

"Yeah," she says, suppressing a smile.

"Yeah."

They sit and look at each other without another word until Liam spots Gwen scoffing mints over by the hostess stand. "So," he says, "let's go get a glow on—as Papa Bear used to say when he thought I wasn't listening—and I'll fill you in on my research."

Everything that is yours, bella.

What is mine, exactly? May wonders, watching Liam walk back from the bar with two foam-topped glasses and a look of triumph on his face. He's close enough to legal back home to get annoyed when they card him, but far enough away, still, to feel proud when they don't. Here nobody seems to care how old—or young—you are. Everyone drinks wine with their kids and thinks nothing of it.

Stashing her phone back in her jacket pocket, May accepts the frosty glass.

"So like I promised, I've been on Google this week." He settles across from her. "There's some interesting stuff out there."

"Like what?"

He raises his glass but sets it down again, laying his hands flat on the round tabletop as if to balance himself. *They're nice hands,* May thinks—for not the first time lately, though she's too distracted and jumpy to consider what that might mean. They're nothing like Marco's hands, but oddly enough, a lot about Liam *does* seem to remind her of Marco. Is she seeing what she wants to see, perhaps, in what's possible?

Liam stretches his long legs under the table and regards the platform stage with an over-satisfied, almost stoned expression. "Well, I was hunting around online and there's this phenomenon called timeslip or retrocognition."

There are no dives in Florence, not like the ones back home, but the café is below street level and dimly lit, with everything, including the stage, painted a dull-black matte. It reeks of beer and would be more at home in Chicago—where Liam and Gwen live now—than Italy, and that must be what he's after.

May lets her gaze drift with his to where the band is starting to set up. It's been nearly an hour, and Liam hasn't looked at his phone once. In fact, it's May who keeps pulling hers out, peering into the glow. There was a text from her mom this morning, and then, at intervals, another and another. Look, *what else can* I *say? I've failed you. I've failed us, and I'm sorry.*

I'm sorry.

I'm sorry.

"And?"

"Some sources describe it as a mass haunting, where you hallucinate places and buildings from the past, sometimes with the associated people. There's a famous case where these two English ladies at the turn of the twentieth century, teachers or a teacher and a principal or something, said they saw Versailles the way it looked in the time of Marie Antoinette."

The drummer is smiling to himself as if he's having an especially nice daydream. He looks high and happy, like he doesn't care much, a bit like Liam tonight. The drummer has a fuzzy goatee and wears a blazer over a clean white T. May looks at him intently, because she can't look that way at Liam, shouldn't look that way at Liam, especially since looking at Liam that way oddly makes her wonder about Marco, what he's doing in his moment in time, in his dank workshop among the dead and dying of another Florence. Would he be like Liam if his life had been easier?

"They wrote a book about it. They were visiting the palace, which is on these vast grounds, and got lost looking for the Petit Trianon. They're wandering around when they start to feel all shitty, like something's oppressing their spirits. Two men in long gray-green coats and triangle hats show up and point them toward the Petit—"

"I'll ask you later what the Petit Whatever is—"

May steals a look at this guy she knows better than anyone, who suddenly feels like a stranger. Her lips feel fat and chapped. She drinks more beer, a lot more beer, and taps her foot along with the sporadic drum warm-up.

The drummer finally leads the band into their first tune, something twangy and moony and hypnotic, and Liam lowers his voice and says, "They come to this isolated cottage where a woman and a girl are standing in funny old clothes, bodicy dresses and whatnot, and the girl's reaching up for a jug the woman's offering."

"A jug?"

"Shh. Listen. So everything goes freeze-frame, like in a movie, and they walk on to a pavilion with something weird and depressing about it—it all sounded pretty glum—and there is this dude sitting outside, his face all messed up from smallpox, wearing a straw hat.

"The man in the hat pays no attention to them, so they walk on quietly and reach a small country house with shuttered windows and terraces on either side. There's a lady on the lawn with her back to the house holding a large board with paper on it, working on a drawing or considering one. She has on a big white hat over her blond hair."

May can almost see them, and the twangy, trancy

music in the background makes for a weird sound track. The man at the table beside them is smoking another cigarette, a mushroom blooming above his head in the stage light.

"A short, poofy dress. A green shawl or kerchief over her shoulders."

"You're not on the witness stand, you know."

Li shushes her, pausing for a long sip, wiping the foam from his mouth. "At the end of the terraces," he goes on, "they see a third house. When they reach it, a door flies open and slams shut again. A young servant comes out, and they file in behind him, nervous all of a sudden that they've trespassed on private property. They follow him back toward the—" He pauses, all expectation.

"Yeah," she obliges. "The Petit Whatever."

"Back home in England, one of our ladies stumbles across this portrait of the queen drawn by some famous artist, and yes, it's the same sketching woman they noticed near—"

"The Petit Trianon—"

"Wearing the same clothes."

It's a good story, May thinks, but it feels like a story. Nothing like Cristofana and Marco or plague sores or a convent full of orphans. She isn't sure how much if any of these particulars Liam is ready to hear. Swirling her beer, May's not sure how willing she is to share them yet. "So what did they do?"

"One of them went back to Versailles in 1902 but couldn't retrace their steps. The grounds looked different. But she also found out that on October fifth, 1789, Marie Antoinette was sitting at the Petit Trianon when word came that a mob from Paris was marching toward the palace."

"OK," May says, closing her eyes to listen. "So what happened?"

"Nothing. I mean, I guess they decided this moment was so emotional and terrible for Marie Antoinette that it just got imprinted there and hung on through the years, and somehow the English ladies stumbled into it. That maybe impressions like this linger, and sensitive people can pick them up. I guess now paranormal investigators call these scenes afterimages.

"A lot of the people who had these timeslips felt like they were in some altered state of consciousness; the air was still and the place seemed mostly silent and abandoned. There's this one thing going on, yeah, but like a loop, over and over, and it's all eerie and depressing."

Eerie and depressing. Again her mind rifles back through all the reading she's been doing, pausing at an image that lodged in her brain that afternoon, an artist's rendering of a plague physician in medieval Europe. Even if you were lucky enough to be seen by a doctor in, say, Florence — most urban docs fled to the countryside or contracted the disease and died — they tended to show up in surreal waxed robes and wide-brimmed hats, big gloves, and this leather mask with glass lenses and a long, scary beak stuffed with vinegar-soaked cloth and spice to distract from your mortal stink.

Cristofana had pointed out one of these nightmare figures on the street once, and May thought she would rather die alone than have that be the last thing she saw. The preferred method of "curing" patients at the time was to bleed them — a slit wrist leaking into a bowl — though doctors might also try a poultice of human excrement or a tonic of diced snake or ground emeralds if you were rich.

It was a bad business, in other words, scary beyond imagining, and May can't grasp the fear and heartbreak Marco and Cristofana must be living with daily. She's seen glimmers of it with her own eyes, but it's not the same. As Cristofana loves to remind her, there's nothing at stake for May. She's a traveler without footprints, a passing phantom.

"Just a little eerie." May looks up. "Yeah."

The band's playing something a little more upbeat,

thank God, though still on the maudlin side. Li swears by what he calls Americana and what everyone else calls country. How did these guys end up in Florence?

And why can't she focus on what Li's saying instead of just his mouth?

"Well, anyway," he goes on, a little self-consciously, picking up on her mood, which he's always done, which used to drive her crazy. "To make a long story short, they're like a loop of film or a videotape, these images, of past stuff linked to some trauma or big event or emotion. You have a lot of battlefield and murder-scene afterimages, of course. Some locations are more conducive than others. Just like some people — ahem, sensitive types — are more likely to pick up on them."

"How's that different from a ghost? In ghost stories, people are always stuck there from another time in old clothes, hanging around for way too long, trying to figure out or avenge or explain something. But they never seem to say much, ghosts, and believe me, Cristofana talks — a lot, all the time — and she *does* affect things, even if I don't. Really, I'*m* the ghost when I'm . . . there."

"Pretty much rules that theory out, then." Li sips his beer, and May smiles at the drummer, who now has a shit-eating grin on his face and seems to be lazily watching their table, though he may just be blinded by a spotlight slicing the room. He took off his jacket between songs, and his freckled arms gleam with sweat.

She turns to Liam, who's looking at her in this drowsy way, and looks away. It's humid in here. No air-conditioning to speak of. Just the one fan, high on the wall, overlooking the swinging kitchen doors.

"There's actual time travel, of course, but that's been disproved by physics and pretty much anyone who hasn't watched too much *Doctor Who*. . . ."

"Like you, for example."

He laughs.

"OK. Why?" she asks as calmly as she can. The more she reads about the Black Death, trying to make sense of what Cristofana's up against—what *she'll* be up against, if Cristofana follows through on her veiled threats—the more agitated May feels.

"Most physicists argue against time travel because it screws with cause and effect." He sips his beer, and, when she raises her eyebrows, adds, "It's a paradox problem. A traveler could go back and kill his grandpa, in which case he'd never be born in the first place. Didn't your parents ever make you watch *Back to the Future*?" Liam always was a sci-fi geek, but as a future physics major, this assignment's right up his alley.

"Right. But what if *when the traveler gets there*," May persists, treading closer to the truth to test his reaction, "she's just a shadow, not flesh and blood? What if she can only watch . . . and can't change anything?"

"Is, um — she — there at all, then?" Liam leans close across the table, his mouth twitching back a smile. "Is that what happens to you?"

A guy at a nearby table blows smoke in their direction, and May wrinkles her nose, trying to ignore the fact that Liam, for all his words to the contrary, is humoring her. This is a pity mission. Maybe he thinks it will score him brownie points. Maybe he thinks it's foreplay.

But I asked him to do it, she thinks, *to humor me*. And because he's obliging, she feels less alone, even if she also feels ridiculous. *But I'm afraid*, Li, she wants to say, though she feels better now, calmer. Better with him. *I'm afraid*.

How can he help her if she's too embarrassed to tell him what's really happening?

"This one guy talks about a kind of quantum theory where everything that can possibly happen, and I mean everything, *is* happening, all the time, in every direction. We think of time like moving water, right? Flowing along. But this guy describes reality more like still images that get linked the way a filmstrip makes a movie. Blink," Liam commands.

She rolls her eyes.

"Seriously. Blink hard, fast, a bunch of times in a row. If every frame of reality is separate, a still—"

"Those stills are in some kind of *order*, Li. And to get from this point to that point takes *time*. Time and reality aren't the same."

"Exactly."

"I don't understand a word you're saying."

"If you buy in, 'reality' is really endless variations, all existing as a series of stills. We may only slot into one 'movie' at a time, but it isn't the only possible one."

"Because we have free will?"

Liam shrugs. "I guess. But it's the time part—time as an absolute in itself—that the theory rejects. Even Einstein called it an illusion, more or less."

May tries to wrap her mind around a slight variation on the scene at hand . . . on a still stacked beside theirs . . . with another on the other side . . . and so on in every direction. All with different outcomes. A heaped jumble like on the tables at a flea market. Some universe.

How many stills away was Cristofana? Worse, how many Cristofana "variations" were there? May has a sudden sharp memory of being small and wobble-ankled on skates, of her mother on one side and her dad on the other, leading her in a figure eight around a frozen pond near Grandma's. "It's the sign for infinity," Dad had explained, and while May didn't know what that meant at the time and didn't feel like spoiling the moment by asking, inviting a lecture, she felt her skinny ankles learning their work, and the easy scrape of blade against ice; she felt her mittened hands in theirs, and the inside of her head spinning round and round, and her body moving forward and back, round and round, over and over, like music. Like forever.

But there is no forever.

Her parents have pointed that out.

As it turns out, time in all its bigness is something May can't fathom. She does better with small. Microbes, which she's been reading about all week, make more sense than the universe, maybe thanks to her brief career as a veterinary intern, maybe because she really just likes this stuff, medical weirdness, but either way, May has been reading and letting her mind dwell on plague, on the reality of it.

What she already knew is that the human body is a colony for microbes, single-celled bacteria so small they can't be seen without a microscope, critters that get picked up in everything we breathe, drink, eat, and touch; they live in hair and mouths and intestines; they groom our eyelashes; and mostly they do it just so they can cop a ride and a little nourishment. All of which is gross, May thinks, but fascinating, too, and normal.

Parasitic microbes, on the other hand, just take, and sometimes kill. They also *spread*—fast—and can infect a lot of people at once. An epidemic. A really *successful* epidemic, one that finds its way around the world, is a pandemic. The Black Death was the beginning of the Second Pandemic. The first toppled the Roman Empire.

One of Gwen's guidebooks explained how historians think bubonic plague hitched a ride with rats from Central Asia to Europe on fleas infected with *Yersinia pestis*, a parasitic microbe. If an infected flea jumped from a rat to a human and took a chomp, it left thousands of microscopic bacteria in the wound. These attacked the lymph nodes, swelling the person's groin and armpits into the "buboes" Cristofana keeps talking about, and causing fever, diarrhea, respiratory distress, and blackened skin. All told, you were usually dead within three days (sooner if you managed to breathe *Yersinia pestis* into your lungs, which gave you hours).

"Then you have supersymmetry—" Liam's saying,

and May juts out her hand like an imperious crossing guard.

"Stop," she demands, closing her eyes, "please, dude." She rubs her temples against the image rising in her mind, a gaping absence, a wall of nothing, leading to a world of nightmares. "I think we nix the paranormal explanation, and while I'm not ruling out crazy physics, my head is going to explode if we don't stop talking about it."

Something in Liam's humid eyes, in the way he looks in that blue stage light at just that moment, makes her suck in air way too fast and blurt out, "Dance with me."

He looks around to see if anyone else is dancing, to see if there's anywhere to dance. They aren't, and there isn't. "Seriously?"

She nods.

"Right. OK. I'm not much of a—"

May stands up before she can change her mind, and she holds out her hand.

He lets her pull him up, lead him to the shadowy edge of a bank of mostly empty tables just below the stage, and drape his right arm around her waist. Leaning forward, she rests her cheek on his shoulder, hands stuffed in the frayed back pockets of his jeans. The drummer is still smiling.

"Why?" Liam whispers into her hair, and she hates that he sounds bewildered.

"Why not?" she says quickly, breathing him in, lifting her face without meeting his eyes, for the first time in a long time thinking not of Marco — who feels remote just now, locked in another age — but of Liam, who smells good, like sweat and aftershave and beer. "You said we should try to have fun while we're over here. Life is good, right?" She rests her lips in the damp curve of his neck, not quite kissing him.

Then the band moves on to some mournful fiddle tune, and Liam leads her back to the table, looking around as if he's just realized where they are. "Look," he says in way too serious a voice, "I'm sure there's some natural phenomenon science hasn't hit on yet that under the right conditions can produce a brief doorway to another time and place. I believe that. I mean, I'm about to major in physics. But the third possibility I mentioned was, well, psychological."

She's about to object when he places two warm fingers to her lips. "Couldn't you just be having some kind of . . . unusual reaction to what's going on at home? To having to make a tough decision and let one of your parents down?"

"Like they haven't let *me* down —"

"I talked to Gwen and —"

"You told Gwen?"

"Just a quick sketch. I'm worried about you, and I can't—"

"You're helping, Li. You're doing your research thing."

Help me, May thinks, afraid to admit she's afraid. *Please.*

He turns his beer glass in his hand, smearing condensation.

"OK, so say I'm nuts. But think about it: those two English ladies were principals or teachers or whatever. They knew about Marie Antoinette. They knew what Paris looked like back in the day. They knew what the clothes and furniture looked like. I hardly knew when the Renaissance happened before I came here."

"But you know a lot now. You've been reading and sightseeing like a maniac. . . ." His voice trails off, for just a second.

"Look. I'm not having some kind of breakdown, if that's what you mean. How could I make all this up or hallucinate in detail what I don't know?"

He stares at her patiently. "You've got an imagination, don't you?"

May shrugs.

"So maybe the history here has wormed into the

back of your head and now you're hallucinating all this because . . ."

"I'm mental?"

"Because you're stressed."

"People who live in Kabul get to be stressed. Starving people in Africa, Kentucky coal miners . . . not some kid from Vermont whose parents are getting divorced while she kills time with her friends in Italy. You've heard the statistics . . . one out of two marriages."

"I know, May. But it's your parents, your life, and that has gravity. For you. We all deal differently with shit, and they're asking you to choose."

"Well said, Dr. Freud."

"We do."

"So you think I need a shrink?"

"Well, from what I'm getting online, shrinks are as nuts as anyone. Killing time ain't the half of it. Carl Jung was a shrink, but I read this morning that when *he* was traveling around Italy in the 1930s, he visited the tomb of some Roman empress in Ravenna. He saw these nice mosaics, all sea and marine scenes, and stood around goggling and talking with his friend about it for like a half hour. When he left the mausoleum, he even tried to purchase postcards of them, but there weren't any. So later, Jung asks a friend who's heading to Ravenna if he'll take a couple pictures for him. When he sees the photos, he gets why no one knew what he was talking about. The mosaics he saw were totally different from the ones there now. They were there, like, seven hundred years earlier, and got destroyed in a fire.

"Jung figured his consciousness had somehow traveled back in time to when the mausoleum had been first constructed, fourteen hundred years prior to his visit to Ravenna. Maybe consciousness gets past the laws of physics somehow. Or maybe you're *imagining* some serious shit here. . . . You've always done that. I mean, I remember when we were little kids, you'd never just sit and play trucks like any normal kid. You always had to invent these worlds and assign everyone names and make costumes. It was freaking exhausting."

Who is he talking about? "I did?"

"You did. You don't remember? Everyone thought you'd grow up to be a director or a general or something, moving all those little flags and troops around on some stage—"

"Well, what about you, with all this sci-fi shit? You've always—"

"Nah. When you come down to it, I have no imagination, I just like it when big lizards fight with big gorillas or whole civilizations are wiped out in some mean fashion by spaceships. It's all about the fight."

"That is such bullshit."

"I know. Go up and get me another beer, will you? Your turn."

"So you're saying I invented all this, like a story."

"Maybe?" He looks sheepish, adding, "But not on purpose," as if that made it OK. "Beer," he pleads, pointing at his glass.

"But what if it's not me? What if I'm not driving this thing but she is?" May looks up, trying to read his face. "What if Cristofana's the one stuck . . . in the middle of the plague and really believes we can trade places? That if I stay, she can leave. She can come here."

"I'm not drunk enough yet to take that in." He looks away almost sadly, drumming his fingers on the table to the music.

She takes the hint, going off in search of more beer.

"I think you may be right," Li continues absently when she returns. "You're losing it." He watches her set down the glasses, his smile pained and mocking. "Which sucks because I can't take advantage of you if you're twitchy in the head. That wouldn't be moral."

"But you heard what Gwen said," May insists, sitting down across from him. "Magic was real to people back then. What if magic is just another word for trading this many atoms for that on the time-space continuum?"

"And Evil You, back in the day, figured all this out by her lonesome without any help from Stephen Hawking? I mean, just because they believed in something doesn't make it true."

May looks away, aware of how all this sounds. "Hey, she's mean but she's not stupid; she's some kind of witch, I think, or sorceress."

"So this witch from the Middle Ages rifles through all the stills in the universe between now and then and figures out how to get back and forth . . . or get you back and forth?"

"Both," May cuts in, and the beer probably is going to her head because why would she tell him all this when he clearly doesn't—can't—believe her?

"Right. Both." He drains his glass, shaking his head. "But if she manages to get here herself, what's she need you for? Why take your place?"

"Because only one of us can be fully present at one . . . in one . . . time. Whoever's visiting turns up a ghost. Useless."

Liam doesn't say anything. They're both quiet for a minute, maybe because the band has just filed offstage for a break, leaving a hollow in the air.

Li wants to believe her. She sees that. He just can't.

"So if suddenly you show up and start kissing me with a whole lot more enthusiasm," he says low, leaning across the table, "I guess I should worry that Evil You has succeeded in her mission?"

When she doesn't answer, Liam wipes beer from his mouth, looking suddenly drawn around the eyes, tired, and she reaches out impulsively and strokes one wolfy eyebrow. *Everything that is yours.*

"Absolutely," she says, and he closes his eyes. "You should."

But her fingers keep moving over his brow until he leans farther over the table, all rakish, opening one blue eye.

Slowly, she draws her hand back. "But on the other hand, that might be me."

The Littlest Sins

See for yourself, traveler.

It's a cruel temptation, this great, invisible hole in her bedroom wall, this silent, beckoning thing with the power to ease May's mind.

Maybe he's dead.

Maybe they both are.

One morning, May wakes up and can't stand it. She needs to be there, *see what's going on*. . . .

No sooner does she emerge in the alley and bolt for the workshop than May spots Cristofana exiting in a sagging embroidered gown the color of peacock feathers. Whoever owned the dress before—a corpse now, no doubt—was taller and heftier than its current owner, who carries the train in her fists as she glides away.

May barely has time to peer between the shutters and drink in the sight of him, alive and well at his easel, before hurrying after her double through winding streets, across the now-familiar bridge, through abandoned fields and August-parched groves, back over the hill to the convent.

This time Cristofana marches right up to the arched wooden door and seizes the knocker, a lion's jaw, rapping it against the iron base. Again, she slips the ruby ring from her finger and drops it into her basket. She looks determined, *too* determined, which makes her seem vulnerable, and May almost feels sorry for her.

A stooped, small woman, not a nun—or at least not in a nun's garb—admits Cristofana, and the huge wooden door clunks closed behind them.

Left on her own, May takes in the terrible hush about the place. The convent wasn't exactly hopping the last time she was here, but there's something different about this silence, dire. She wavers a minute, thinking like flesh and bone, before it occurs to her that she's in ghost form and can pass through the wall, which she does, wishing immediately that she hadn't.

The long room she ends up in, exposed in shadows (though if a ghost is going to look at home anywhere, it's here), is a house of horrors. Here and there a candle or spitting torch cuts the gloom. The shadows are deep but can't conceal the crazy quilt of women and children, nuns and orphans, turning and tossing on piled straw, row after jagged row of makeshift cots. May floats quickly into a partially open wardrobe, careful not to jut through the wood as she watches through the crack. A sick antiseptic smell fills the room, boiled herbs and vomit, and the thick stone walls look as if they're sweating, though it's chill inside, deathly chill for the middle of an Italian summer. The sound of too many people groaning and trying not to be heard makes for a muffled roar.

May cringes a little as Sister Arcangela, making rounds, crosses very close, kneeling by a child with a sleeping baby in its arms. Cristofana follows behind, looking wary and tired, and May ducks back farther into the damp gloom of the wardrobe.

The orphans in the nuns' care have been dying, Marietta reports under her breath, one by one, infecting the sisters in the meantime. "Come sit by me," she urges, her eyes hollow in the candlelight. Cristofana steps nearer but stiffens when her sister adds, "Better yet, kneel, sister, bend to His will. There is peace in it."

Kneeling seems almost as hard for Cristofana as being in this room in the first place, which shouldn't surprise May but still does.

"He is one of the youngest," her sister explains. "Just a month old. Left on our doorstep as most of them are. See here?" She gestures with her chin, lifting the edge of the infant's blanket, letting it fall. "The sickness shows first in the groin or armpits. The tumors, *gavoccioli*, are the size of eggs, oranges sometimes. Here, take the cloth. Cool them."

At that Cristofana draws the line, moving away from the damp scrap of linen as if it might bite her. "I came only to say good-bye—"

"You already said good-bye," Marietta reminds her curtly. She strokes the older child's forehead with the wadded cloth. "Do you know that Benedetta carried her infant brother all the way here from a village near Scandicci? He died before they arrived, and the only way we could console her was to give her this one instead. She doesn't seem to know the difference. This child—" she begins, her voice filling with warmth.

"Is not my child. I did not come here to forsake my life but to ask your forgiveness for saving it."

"It is not my forgiveness you require, sister."

"Whose, then? Let me guess."

The nun continues stroking her patient's damp

forehead with the cloth, her voice grave. "They are lost or failing, the other sisters, and apart from loyal Maria, Mother Abbess's niece, I care for these alone." The girl, Benedetta — May wouldn't have been able to tell its gender on her own; the child's hair is cropped and her face wasted and pale — seems to spasm then, rolling on her side, coughing blood with a wet *splat* over the baby onto the nun's veil. As Sister Arcangela eases the bundle from her arms, Cristofana winces and backs away on her knees, out of reach, out of the candle's glow, partly obscuring herself in shadow. She stands up, and she might be trembling — May can't tell at this angle — but she's definitely agitated, rocking slightly, wild-eyed, a caged animal compared to her stoical sister.

The nun sets the sleeping infant aside on a blanket, ignoring the mark on her veil. She wipes a red string of saliva from Benedetta's mouth, stroking the narrow, veined wrist with her fingers until the girl is soothed to sleep. Then she rises and moves to another patient nearby, with Cristofana standing back, her reluctant shadow. "As the buboes spread," she resumes like a lecturer, pointing out sections of a dying child's body with her voice low and mechanical, "the malady changes. Black or livid spots blaze on the arms and thighs, now few and large, now small and numerous. It was hard at first, to feel anything but revulsion, for this disease degrades as well as kills. It turns the breath foul and the urine to blood-black sludge. There is another chain of sickness, too, which you saw, marked by the coughing of blood. With the tumors, you die in five days or six — though some few survive and recover. Those who spit blood never do." She glances back at Benedetta. "These die in a day or two, three at most. The majority here will not be alive by the Sabbath. Even those who yet show no signs."

May follows the line of the sister's raised arm. Across the room, on a large straw pallet, the ones who must still be healthy curl together, twitching in their sleep, their bare ankles bony and pale.

"As I wash their small bodies for burial, shocked every time by the black blotches, the fierce swellings, I wonder who washed Babbo's body aboard ship. Was it Ludovico who folded him into whatever passed for a clean sheet? Did he do as I do here, tracing black crosses on tiny shrouds with a cooled stick from the embers?

"Even the littlest sins can stain the soul, and through no fault of their own, Babbo and all these multitudes are denied the ministrations of a priest. There are no holy men left to bless them, just as in the end there were none aboard ship to bless our father.

"I see it in my sleep, Sire dragged away in chains, his soul snatched by grinning demons. I hear him . . . the wailing as he's hurled into the inextinguishable fires of Hell—"

Cristofana lets out her own wail of aggravation. "I beg you, sister. What God is this?"

"If our father knew how your faith has waned—"

"Bless him, but you speak continually of Babbo and never once ask after Mamma or what became of us in his absence and yours. You live so near Firenze and heard nothing of our misery?"

Marietta seems taken aback. Startled. "My vows preclude the world without."

Cristofana waves. "The world without has found its way in."

"My eyes have been rinsed in the blood of the lamb and see only His love."

Shaking with frustration or rage, Cristofana blurts out, "Mamma is dead. She lay in a pool of *her* blood for hours before anyone came."

Sister Arcangela looks up with the eyes of someone who can no longer be surprised. Crossing herself, she murmurs, "And you?"

"Left for dead . . . rescued by our neighbor, the midwife—you remember; 'the witch Callista' we called her when we were small. She raised me as her own, and I am like her now. Your God disgusts me."

With blank eyes, Sister Arcangela begins chanting what May thinks is the Hail Mary. Her blank voice, rising in strength and pitch, only seems to infuriate Cristofana, who sinks to her knees and starts rocking forward and back. "The Virgin is deaf and dumb! The Holy Mother is deaf and dumb and the Holy Father, too. They are nowhere." She tips forward, knocking her forehead hard against stone, making May wince. "Nowhere," she repeats weakly, her tangle of hair fanned around her. "And we are nothing."

May is momentarily tempted to go to her in her sister's stead and calm her — some of the figures on the floor have turned their hollow eyes toward Cristofana's voice — but like Sister Arcangela, May can only watch Cristofana cry herself quiet.

In a moment, she rises unsteadily, adjusting her peacock gown (more modest than the plum one, though still outlandish in this place). The nun won't look at her but stops chanting, poised in the moment, waiting for her sister's next move.

Cristofana backs away slowly. "You have always saved the best of yourself for strangers," she says. Though her head is bowed, the words ring distinctly, and she sidesteps the zigzag of straw cots, disappearing into the dark of the corridor.

Sister Arcangela smooths her veil, steps over the recent corpse of a child to kneel by one who's living, and begins a silent prayer.

Ninna-oh

Home again and safe, May spends the next morning, Sunday, skulking by the Arno as the bells of Florence peal.

She follows the river farther than she has before, leaving the city limits, it seems, leaving everything. If Li's timeslip theory from the bar makes any sense (and it doesn't, really), she's supposed to find the *past* eerie and depressing, not the present, but May can't escape what she witnessed at the convent. Not even here.

A hazy sun is cresting the rise, and May lets the morning fog have her, a damp embrace. Calm one minute and panicked the next, she steps farther in, snared in the strangeness of her own mood. The entire riverbank is obscured, and she with it. Who will find her ever again? She'll vanish off the face of the earth, like those numberless plague dead Cristofana is always talking about. The dead and dying May has now seen with her own eyes.

"Look, *bella*," comes that level voice, floating out from the fog, reeling May in, and at first she doesn't trust that what she's hearing is real. "Come look what I've found."

Ghost Cristofana steps from the yellow tendrils of fog with a ghost baby in her arms, a large one swaddled in a too-small blanket. "I found her alone in all the world. She has not words, but she loves my voice. Listen."

The baby's hollowed cheeks puff in and out as it sucks furiously on Cristofana's milky-faint index finger.

Healthy, May thinks. *Thank God*.

"If I do not sing or stuff my finger in its craw, it howls like a demon."

"It's hungry." May reaches to touch the downy ghost forehead in that automatic way you do when someone holds a baby under your nose, but her hand passes through. "It needs milk."

"And you have some?" Cristofana snaps. "No, nor

do I. If there is a wet nurse anywhere in our foul city, she is busy with every orphan from here to Pisa." Pursing her lips at the creature, Cristofana croons, "Isn't that so, *ninna-oh?*"

"Then go find her, this nurse."

"You think yourself fit to order me about like a mistress? Do you suppose you have the florin to pay for my service?"

Patiently, as if speaking to someone on the ledge of a tall building, May lowers her voice. "Let me help, Cristofana. Just listen. That's all I ask." She takes in a sharp breath. "Bring her to the convent."

Cristofana's eyes lock on her, intense and frightening. She steps close, bouncing the baby in her spectral arms. "What did you say?"

"I said bring her to the convent." May's voice cracks under the strain of her twin's puzzled, disbelieving stare. "Yes, I know about your sister. She'll help you. Bring the baby there." May shudders at the thought, remembering the place, the smell and the despair. "With the other orphans."

"I see I am not the only one who sneaks and studies." Cristofana's grim expression lets up, as if she's gained newfound respect for May, but her voice is furtive. "I could bring this there, but why? It amuses me. Watch."

She removes her finger from the baby's mouth and

tickles the child's dimpled chin with it, her voice warbling in a way that's almost comical for its gentleness.

> "*Baby, baby, naughty baby,*
> *Hush, you squalling thing, I say.*
> *Peace this moment, peace, or surely*
> *Death will pass this way.*"

May takes in the sweep of the riverbank. The fog is a patchwork, and ahead in a clear patch she sees where Cristofana likely came through, a dim alley leading back up to the crooked cart roads of the old city.

The riverside, what she can make out of it, is deserted, desolate. Despair wells up in her. May knows she won't be able to reach out and rescue the baby, just as she couldn't snatch the kitten from the bucket, just as she couldn't reach for Marco after that first time (lips, skin, longing). "Please." Her pleading voice sounds cracked and feeble. "Just think about it. Don't let her die."

Cristofana isn't listening. She's rocking the baby almost tenderly, breathing her vitriol into its entranced face.

> "*Baby, baby, he's a giant,*
> *Tall and dark as our cathedral,*

And he nibbles, don't you know,
Every day on naughty people."

"This isn't a kitten," May pleads, "and someone will care for it. Someone will. Marietta will. Just don't—"

"Don't what?" her twin demands, eyes flashing. "Don't tease? Don't sing? Don't play or smile or breathe a word except of sorrow?" Defiant—in the face of *what*, May can't say: death itself, perhaps—her eyes almost wounded, Cristofana spits. May winces, but her cheek is dry when she wipes it. "Will *you* come care for it, *bella*?"

"You know I can't."

"Oh, but you can." Cristofana purses her lips, sneering. "The question is, *will* you? Perhaps Marco is not enough for you. But like my sister, you are a saint in your own mind. Surely you, who would save all the animals and nurse the sick, wish to help this poor child. Surely you have a conscience, like Marietta, who dooms herself nursing other people's children."

"I'm sorry," May offers, and she is, though she doesn't know Sister Arcangela. The woman strikes her as cold and distant, at least to Cristofana, but there's probably a good reason for that, and the sister formerly known as Marietta is apparently all the girl has left in the world.

Not true, May thinks, feeling her eyes brim with frustrated tears. Because now Cristofana's found herself a baby. Perhaps it even came from the convent, from among the last survivors. If it's come to that. "What happened?" she asks as gently as she can. "Where did you find her?"

Cristofana is humming wildly under her breath, like the crazy bag lady May remembers from some movie, who finds a doll in an abandoned parking lot and rocks it, sings to it, won't let anyone take it from her. She ignores May's question completely.

"Tell me something," May tries. "You're here now . . . more or less, with this baby. Why not just go back, get Marco, and all three of you come through the portal together? Just wait it out. When the plague passes, you go home again. With them." May can't believe her own words, can't believe she's giving Marco away like that, as if he's hers to give.

"Wouldn't that be convenient for you and your precious conscience?" Cristofana shakes her head as if to clear it. "There is no telling how long the Pest will stay. Even before, many in my Firenze would not live to see their children grow. Mothers die birthing them. Babes do not survive childhood. I loathe death, above all things, and as I stand here with my head aching—without blood, flesh, or hunger—the sands pour through the hourglass. My life is flying now, like a bird, and I will not trade on it any longer than I have to."

May thinks of her own last real visit to Marco in the workshop, that ghost loneliness. As hard as the feeling was for May to endure, it must be unbearable for Cristofana, whose will and appetites are so obvious. "But it's all beside the point if you're dead," May argues. "Why don't you just trick me, then?" she says, laying it out there. "Or force me to make this trade you keep talking about? What are you waiting for? You don't seem like you're above that kind of thing."

Cristofana tilts her head, a wild look in her eyes, like someone hearing voices in her head, voices growing louder and more insistent by the minute. "I want from you only the life you would otherwise waste." She circles May, lulling the poor baby under her breath with that sick nursery tune. "You sulk and resist, and I can't but wonder if you have a right to life at all, as I do. As this hungry child does."

Stunned and somehow resigned, May whispers, "Just don't hurt it."

"It is a she, *bella*. Pippa, who knows her name. Don't you, duck?" Cristofana tickles the grinning baby. Saliva pools in the dirty creases around the heart-shaped mouth. "She has a little locket to prove it."

One dimpled baby hand gropes and smacks at Cristofana's face while a lazy eye fixes sideways on May. She's an ugly, battered-looking kid, about eleven months old. Fat and gangly, worried and trusting—even in shadow form, there is something funny and sweet about Pippa, and May feels a strange affection for her.

"*Baby, baby, if he hears you*
As he gallops past the house,
Limb from limb at once he'll tear you,
Just as kitty tears a mouse."

The word *kitty* works its rough magic, and May shudders as if drenched in cold water, realizing she's lost sight of Cristofana, who has wandered off into the fog with her prize. May feels it again—that now-familiar, impossible urge to reach, to alter something—and snaps to, angry at herself for being lulled again into trusting Cristofana. *I hate you*, she thinks, stepping back into a rank yellow fog that reminds her of illness, and though May can no longer see her shadow double, for a while she still hears her and stands very still, like prey, listening.

"*And he'll beat you, beat you, beat you.*"

May can't see her own hand in front of her, and her compass is thrown. "Don't hurt her, Cristofana!" she yells, her voice echoing all around.

"And he'll beat you all to pap."

When the voice sounds again, it is already far away.

"And he'll eat you, eat you, eat you,
Every morsel, snap, snap, snap."

The Alchemist

Cristofana was wise to leave the portal there, in May's room, a gaping mouth with a siren's song in its throat. A mousetrap.

May can't help but muse on this as she comes and goes, regarding that unused back corner of her room and the gaping presence there that feels like absence. What *if* a mouse . . . or some other animal . . . a plague-ridden vagrant, for example, scavenging in the alley marked with a sideways 8 (or Gwen or Liam, for that matter, on this side of time), darted or stumbled or swooped through, like Cristofana's hapless bird? Never to be seen again in their own age. Cristofana obviously knew to isolate her portal points, but someone *could* happen through. Someone might.

Vowing it won't be her, not voluntarily, May takes the next few days to catch up on tasks for Gwen, staying out of her room, staying busy: chasing down photo permissions and quote attributions, photographing restaurant fronts and gravestones with Gwen's digital camera, taking a day to bus over to Oltrarno to visit Palazzo Pitti and Boboli Gardens, waiting in line at archives.

There's no way to destroy the portal, a structure she can sense but not see. There's nothing visible there for May to work out, no tangible clue, apart from the weird mirrored fabric she once saw Cristofana use to close it down, and there's the dim possibility that her twin might be too caught up in her conflict with Marietta and the demands of a baby to seriously think of leaving Old Florence.

Either way, May's last and only option is to stay clear, avoid getting caught on the wrong side of time. No more risky outings. No more curiosity. No more pity. No more Marco.

She's afraid to stay in her room, afraid of what might echo out from that blankness—what pleas, demands, or horrors—so she moves out that weekend to the front room, transfers her laptop, research books, and magazines to the glass coffee table, keeps her clothing in her suitcase on the floor, and starts sleeping on the striped, satiny couch. *Out of sight, out of mind, right?*

But he isn't. He isn't. None of it is, though May persists in believing otherwise.

Gwen and Liam don't say a word. They must figure that May thinks her room's haunted again. And it is, in a way. She is. By guilt and longing, mostly. Marco seems like a promise the world retracted, and the loss, the not knowing what's become of him or what they might have been, is a cruel torture. May has never in her life, for a moment, felt tragic, but her decision to stay away, stay safe, feels like tragedy in that grand sense, the way Shakespeare meant it. (After this, she's mused more than once, choosing which parent to live with will be easy: Mom. Dad. Dad. Mom . . .)

Knowing what's behind the closed door of her bedroom has an almost magnetic attraction for May, and she's actually relieved about a week into her resolution when Gwen lays out some dozen tourist pamphlets on the table at breakfast. "What's your pleasure? We need to jar ourselves out of routine here. I haven't been up to Fiesole yet. But maybe you two are ready for Siena or Rome now, or Venice?"

May and Liam sit on their stools, scraping spoons in cereal bowls, each waiting for the other to answer.

They stayed up way too late watching on-demand, and Liam's still wearing his clothes from last night. They haven't talked much—since the bar—about May's episodes, partly because his questions trailed off and May began to understand that it was making him uncomfortable, not being able to believe her when he wanted to so badly.

These days it's almost as if she's forgotten how to distinguish waking from sleep, flesh from nightmare, but she remembers well enough the smell of Liam's T-shirt while they were dancing that night, the slight heat off his skin, and the good, simple feeling of safety. She feels herself blushing now, wondering if it can ever happen again. If it ever will.

"Come on, you two. I know you had another late night, but I won't have you going home to the States with nothing to show for yourselves. I seem to recall journal entries and essays need to be written. You can't write about sitting up all night watching bad action movies."

"My English teacher would be all for it," Liam tries. "'A real writer,' he's always saying, 'makes something out of nothing.' 'Heaven in a grain of sand,' right?"

Gwen levels him with a look. "You think you're going to impress me by quoting Blake?"

"Yes?" Liam slurps up some milk from his bowl of

Weetabix — Gwen's a fiend for Weetabix — wearing a white mustache with his smile. "Distract you, at least."

"Your father was always handy with a quote. One for every occasion. I never knew if he was mocking me or not." It's impossible not to pick up the subtle shift in Gwen's voice, from amused to bitter. "He had a way of making a person feel pretentious."

May can tell by the way Liam looks down, stirring the soggy flakes left in his bowl, that this is in the category of Too Much Information. Did Gwen date after Billy left? It's a weird idea, even weirder in a way for May than her own mom dating. Both Gwen and May's mom seem to live in their heads. Did you get old and just stop sharing yourself that way? Or will May have to deal with a stepfather or stepmother? Or worse — siblings? She'd always wanted brothers and sisters when she was young. But not like this. And that was then.

"I have a question. What's a wet nurse?" she demands, in a voice that suddenly seems way too loud.

Gwen smiles, her gaze intent. "A lactating mother who nurses another woman's baby. Often a servant or a peasant hired by a wealthy woman who can't be bothered to do it herself. You don't hear the term much anymore."

"*Lactating* is not a word I hope to hear again *any*-time. *Ever.*" Liam winces, raising an arm as if against a blow when they turn scolding looks on him. He walks his bowl to the sink, rinses it, and turns to the window. When he speaks again, his voice is cheerful enough but far from kidding. "I'm bored, Ma."

His mother abruptly clears butter dish, jam, and fruit bowl from the table. Her sigh goes on forever, and she actually looks angry. "You know me pretty well, Liam, and you know boredom's one sin I won't tolerate. You can drink beer or cuss or bring home the occasional C in calc, but you can't, you don't *dare*, look me in the eye and admit to being bored. Not here. Not anywhere. Stupid people are bored. People with no imagination."

May looks away, embarrassed for him.

"Ouch," Liam goes on, "that's harsh. But May's bored, too. Aren't you, May? Work with me here."

"No," May says. "I just feel disconnected sometimes, left out, like I'm missing the point. Like a tourist, I guess . . . and not just because I'm in Italy. Does that make sense?" It feels weird, admitting this, but Cristofana, who hardly knows her, sometimes knows more about May than May does.

Gwen smiles. "It makes perfect sense. I often feel the same way—especially when I travel—until I find myself in some conversation or landscape that reminds me why I came and brings me back to wonder."

"Please don't get her going about wonder and imagination." Liam groans. "Then it'll be Einstein and on and freaking on." He turns to May. "Here's why Dad had to go around groveling and quoting Great Thinkers all the time."

May shrugs, so he turns back to Gwen. "Can't we quote Lady Gaga instead? Or SpongeBob? I'd like to talk about SpongeBob."

He's kidding, May thinks, but he isn't, and part of her understands . . . part of her wants to be lying on the rug on Saturday morning watching cartoons, with a milk mustache and a bowl of Lucky Charms at her elbow and True licking the last of the milk out of the bowl. No relics or divorces or essays to write, or phantom lovers or babies to rescue from sociopathic doppelgängers when you're not physically in the same layer of time. May rubs what she imagines are dark circles under her eyes with her thumbs.

Gwen reaches out, lifting her chin. "I'm curious," she says. "What made you ask about a wet nurse?"

May looks at Liam, who shrugs as if to say, *You're on your own with this one*. "I had another bad dream, I guess."

"About a wet nurse?" Gwen's trying not to smile. "That's, well . . . different."

"Not exactly *about*."

Gwen's digging in now, looking too hard at first one and then the other of them, so May knows she'd better tie this up. "What I'd like to do today is learn more about the plague here in the fourteenth century. I'm writing one of my essays about it, remember? The one for history."

Gwen's face lights up. "I've got just the place, then. I know a museum with an interactive exhibit. . . . A microcosm of medieval life, at least as the underclasses lived it. The exhibit's a bit sensational, but it gets its point across. I came when I was here last time."

"A little microcosm is just what I need," May says, looking at Liam, who rolls his eyes. "Right, Li? 'Heaven in a grain of sand'?"

"More like Hell," Gwen adds, her voice matter-of-fact and chilling. "And the exact lines are 'To see a world in a grain of sand, / And heaven in a wild flower.' Has anyone seen my other hiking boot?"

"'Through interactive guides, films, and images,'" Gwen reads from the guidebook, "'the display creates a picture of life as endured by those men and women not born to wealth and noble privilege,' *blabbity blabbity*, 'an existence characterized by injustice, disease, and filth. Here the republicanism and' *blabbity blabbity* 'for which Florence was famous were nowhere in evidence.

Law and punishment were dispensed by the rich at the expense of the poor; those with money paid; those without were executed.'"

When they arrive, Liam more or less camps out in a room full of torture devices, while May and Gwen continue on past a re-created market cart stocked with typical Florentine fare of the day—most of which the average peasant could only salivate over, an interactive audio explains in Italian, English, German, and Japanese—and, finally, past a room devoted to medieval medical and dental practices and diseases like leprosy and, yes, the plague.

Though May can't help comparing the audio and what she reads on the placards to what she's seen, she's too distracted to form an opinion either way, though Gwen keeps soliciting one.

Next up is a reconstructed peasant dwelling, an underground building with no windows or light coming in from the outside. The ceilings are barely five feet high, and it's humid as hell inside. The audio guide says that in real life the house would be teeming with vermin, parasites, and the stench of human waste. Here again, in the back of her mind, May can't help comparing these models to the real thing and wonders all over again what's real and what isn't, wonders—at mention of parasites—if her dad is remembering to give

True his worm meds every month and check him for ticks.

More or less exhausted by worry over her dog and her parents and herself and Marco, and now, in a surreal twist, this baby—Pippa—May ducks out of Gwen's sight line into a sideline display on medieval magic.

In the arched cave of the film nook, she sits on the rug-covered bench alone in the dark for three full loops of a mini documentary on alchemy. The man on-screen is dressed like a wizard. He's seated at a big table lined with fat leather volumes, floaty dead things in jars, and liquids bubbling in beakers, neat and tidy enough to be a little museum display in its own right. The man's robe is a spotless royal purple, and the big fire burning in the hearth behind him makes the whole thing feel a bit like *Masterpiece Theatre* on dope. The tour's in English because May got to choose her language, but the voice actor's Scottish or something, and she can barely understand what he's saying. His voice is deep and slow, persistent like flowing water, both soothing and unsettling. "Step lightly," the Italian-Scottish alchemist urges, looking straight at her, and here's what's wrong: his face is flickering, bleeding into someone else's.

"Close your eyes." May hears it distinctly now,

Cristofana's muffled voice sounding under the drone of the audio tour, familiar and teasing. One minute it's the Scottish dude talking, and the next it's Cristofana. One minute the camera pans over his orderly table, and the next, the witch presides over a mockery of the theatrical set. Part spilled contents of a crazy bag lady's shopping cart, part jumbled secondhand store, part withered garden, her table has bottles and books, just as his does. But it's also heaped with dusty objects of every sort—the scraps, bits, and bobs of a scavenger. Her robe is a mockery, too, a crazy-quilt of stolen brocade and peasant sack, silk and rags, jewels and feathers.

The Cristofana-wizard is holding up a large, clear jar with a little doll slumped inside, made of some kind of hairy root with a lock of dirty-blond hair tied on top with twine.

"Come," he says—or she does, flickering, crooning—"and cheat time with me. I have your poppet here, see? In this glass. Do as she does. Move as she moves. Little You."

Little Me. It could as easily be Cristofana, though. *We correspond.*

"What *is* that thing?" May asks out loud.

"*Mandragora officinarum*, also known as Satan's apple, Circe's plant, dudaim, ladykins, manikin . . ."

The words themselves ring like a spell, and May wonders if she's being enchanted. Her head feels light and her eyes blur in the cool dark of the deserted exhibit. Where are Gwen and Liam?

"The mandrake came of the same clay as Adam," the wavering voice says, "and so the Devil holds it in great favor. If grown beneath the gallows, or where suicides lie buried at a crossroads, it is powerful indeed." He-she smiles absurdly wide, white teething glimmering. "You must go at sunset or in the dead of night and loose the earth. With the point of a two-edged sword that has never drawn blood, scratch three circles around the plant to stop the demons from rising with the root. You have meanwhile tied a black dog — a starved animal is best — to the stalk with a stout cord. Stand back with a trumpet to your lips and hurl meat out of the animal's reach. Aim carefully, and he'll lunge and tear the root from the earth. But beware, *bella*. Make a shrill blast with your trumpet, for when you pull it up, the mandrake sounds a shriek that brings death to all who hear it."

Earplugs, anyone? "Including the poor starved dog," May complains, thinking of True, of the kitten. The Middle Ages were no place for hapless animals, it seems, no place for anyone.

"The foolish crave ladykins for their love potions

and flying ointments, so I am not above improvising." Cristofana-wizard gropes a loose manikin from her piles. "A bit of poisonous bryony root is a brave substitute. Carve it roughly into human shape. Attach a seed of barley or millet to both head and chin. Bury the root for several weeks, and you'll see the seed sprout, appearing like so. Amazing! No knife marks. Note how the new tissue has grown over. I challenge you to distinguish it from any true mandrake or womandrake.

"Now, then. Wash the root in wine. Bind it in silk and velvet. Feed it . . . with sacramental wafers stolen from a church during Communion . . . and you have your manikin."

Abandoning her bryony forgery, Cristofana-wizard lifts the jar and displays Little Me on her palm, pivoting it for the camera in a way that would make Home Shopping Network proud. "But I took every precaution," she concludes, "in your case."

"Are you ADD or what?"

"They say that to imprison an imp in a bottle rattles its wits," she goes on. "Over and over it will change shape, anxious to escape, but the bottled imp will perform all manner of miracles for its master. It will divine gold and cause mischief for his enemies." She sighs morosely. "Which bodes well, but your poppet will not play. This does not rule you or anyone else."

She sets down the jar and extends her hand, which seems to reach from the screen in 3-D, the ruby in her gold ring glinting. "Even still, I have my ring. You will come peacefully, yes?"

"Ring?" May asks, confused, for now the actor playing a medieval Italian alchemist is yammering in his lilting Scottish accent about a philosopher's stone, the elixir of life, about universal cures, potions, and powders . . . about drinkable gold and a ring that might make its wearer invisible or give him two bodies at once.

"Yes, you remember her. The girl with the ruby, the finger I sawed away?"

The voice is blurring now, and the face fading in and out. "You asked for a spell, and here I have one. It is my own favorite, *bella*. Do you have your quill, as my first master used to say? He was a seer, one who closed his eyes and groped into the dark as I do, but his visions sought only artifacts, those imbued with special meaning by God or his disciples. He was a materialist who would reach back in time and gather all the great objects of biblical lore, dusty shrouds and coins and vessels, but he never thought to look into the future, *bella*, where I found you. He never watched his back, either, though when he died, he placed this ring on his daughter's finger — she was all he had left, though

I was more his sort than she was—thinking it would render her invisible and keep her safe (from me, perhaps). But the ring has another use. It can grant the wearer two bodies. And so we are two, you and me. Are you ready? Here it is. Your spell:

"Tit for tat
This for that
Here for there
Now for then
Amen."

"Are you telling the truth?" May asks, afraid of the answer, her head reeling, unreal. "Even a little?"

Cristofana throws back her head and laughs uproariously. She doesn't stop laughing for what seems like a long time, and in that time the room grows cold and small. It becomes a room again, with edges and shadows, with the murmur of museumgoers beyond walls.

"No," she says. "It's a lie, of course, every word. How silly you are, *bella*, to indulge me at such length."

"Why do you do this?" May whispers, feeling nuts again.

"Do what?"

"Mess with me?"

"Because you amuse me. Because I don't want to

die, and you can help me, and because you won't . . . help me."

"How does the portal work? Show me."

"The time of negotiating is past." Cristofana-wizard flickers. "Haven't you wondered about him after all these days, *bella*? About the baby? Do they live or die? Have I cut Marco's pretty throat or drowned Pippa in a horse trough? Has the Pest curled outside our doorstep like a dragon, lapping its lips? Your silence surprises me greatly."

May feels her breath catch, though she doesn't believe it. Not really. Any of it. She *can't* believe it. *We share the same soul.*

"You doubt me?" Cristofana challenges, leaning forward on-screen. If May were wearing 3-D glasses, her double would leap out at her, a boogeyman with her own face. "But how can this be? You know I like my playthings . . . kittens and dollies." She lifts Little Me from its jar and slowly plucks the long blond hair from its lumpen head, leaving only baby fuzz. "You are a good little nun. Come and care for her . . . Pippa . . . before she is beyond care."

May can't speak. Her tongue lies like lead in her mouth. As if to relieve her, the Italian-Scottish wizard starts humming under his breath again, jarring her. "Maybe we can figure out how to get you out," May blurts, "all three of you. There must be a way . . . without my having to play human sacrifice."

"There is no way. Believe me. Time will be tricked—a bird for a bird—but never cheated. We are waiting," Cristofana says, flickering again. "You must know you are her only hope."

"*Every morsel,*" sings the wizard in his lilting Scottish accent, "*snap, snap, snap.*"

"Don't make me come for you."

May is suddenly acutely aware of smells and sounds. Peanut butter and Liam, who has found her and skootched her over on the rug bench with his hip, parking himself half lotus–style. "Let's get the hell outta Dodge," he whispers, sneaking spoonfuls of peanut butter from the jar in his backpack. She leans sideways to breathe him in, tempted to rest her forehead on his shoulder, but instead, instinctively, they inch apart. Gwen can't be far behind, though no one has ever stopped Gwen from figuring things out—and what "things" is May even worrying about?

She's struck hard by a vision of that poor baby, Cristofana's latest plaything, writhing on the dirt floor of the workshop, startled and screaming, abandoned to the wolves. The child is just part of Cristofana's plan, May knows. She's using them all—Marco, too, by this point—in some game beyond their understanding.

But her twin can't do more than bluff, May knows. Cristofana can plague her all she wants, threaten, berate—even without help from the portal, as her alchemist gig proves—but can't lay a hand on her. Because they can't both be real here at the same time.

As long as May resists going through the portal of her own accord, she'll be OK. Safe.

When she thinks of Pippa wailing with hunger, of Marco's deepening sadness and confusion, she has to wonder if safety's all she's always cracked it up to be.

The idea of changing places again, even briefly, is terrifying. Most terrifying of all, she thinks, giving in to the spoonful of peanut butter Liam holds out for her, is what might happen to him and to Gwen if Cristofana got loose in the present. *Everything that is yours,* bella.

Better Than Most

The moment May enters her stuffy, closed bedroom, ostensibly to retrieve her Italian phrase book, she knows she's made the mistake of a lifetime.

Being this close, feeling its gaping, invisible presence, knowing how easy it would be to go through only makes it seem physically necessary, inevitable, and maybe it is. Maybe May only imagined she had a choice.

You have a choice. Isn't that what May told Cristofana? So righteous and indignant. *So sure of yourself*—as Li put it—*your tidy little world.*

May stands transfixed by the wall, imagining Marco gaunt at his easel, clawing with a stick of charcoal, his face smudged with it, the paper alive with writhing and screaming, with the pains of Hell and the madness of innocence, and she so much wants to watch the image on that easel come to life. She wants to be there when he makes it, be a part of his story, however terrible, and to share and soothe and be seen. She can almost see the veins in his strong, long hands leaping with the work, his eyes possessed, and she imagines, with hope, what he would do when he looked up and found her there, May in the flesh, as real as stone and bone and water.

But what kind of idiot would she be, to go back there now?

Liam looks in later and finds her trancing on the bed with the phrase book open on her lap — one her mom supplied, along with guidebooks and art books, the night before they dispatched May for the summer.

"What's up?"

She knows he's there, but his voice jars her, and she starts thumbing through the pages again. "What's it look like?" she asks. *Touch. You. Twin. Danger.*

He shrugs. "Um . . . I don't know. That's why I asked."

"Learning Italian."

Liam sits down beside her, and the swaying mattress makes her blush. "Makes sense. But I kinda thought we were of the ignorance-is-bliss school, since pretty much everyone here speaks enough English to get us by."

"Everyone here now."

"Got it." He sighs. "What's really up?"

May takes a deep breath, plunging in. "The plague is on full force there. The only other person left in her family is either dead or about to be, and Cristofana's running out of reasons to stay." Right now her restless twin could be anywhere, raiding the stores in some old farmhouse, dressing up in other people's clothes, dead people's clothes, wearing their jewelry, reading their books, murdering their kittens, but wherever she is, she isn't happy. Her plaything Pippa could likewise be anywhere, left by the wayside, parched and frightened, flies at her eyes. "Look, I can't explain now, but if I disappear for a bit . . . cover for me? Tell Gwen I met up with a friend from home, and we're gonna backpack around and hostel it for a few days?"

"She won't buy it."

"I know, but do it anyway."

"You're freaking me out."

"I can't help it, Li. I'm sorry." She touches his cheek quickly, hating the pity in his eyes. He thinks she's losing it, and maybe she is. Or not. There's only one way to find out.

"Let me go with you," he says softly. "Wherever you're going."

She wants to kiss him, but this isn't the time, and maybe there never will be a time, and she isn't doing him any favors pretending otherwise. Time is very definitely the problem. "I don't know when it will be," she says. "I don't know if . . . I'll be able to get back. Just cover for me, OK?"

"May," he pleads, "you said you'd talk to someone if—"

"And if *I* turn up and seem strange, all sly and evil and shit, then—"

"You said you'd talk to someone," he repeats flatly.

"I'm talking to you."

"Someone qualified."

She pauses, annoyed, thumbing briskly through the phrase book again. What if she found a way to explain—about the plague and how it worked, how to cure it—to a doctor of Marco's day?

On the one hand, Liam's *Back to the Future* paradox makes sense, and what could May possibly trade for a historic game changer like antibiotics? How would she strike that famous balance Cristofana keeps talking about? Impossible. There is no trade big enough, and anyway, May doesn't need or want to save the world. . . . Just one life or two—three if she's feeling generous. She's not that good, despite what Cristofana might think.

On the other hand, it may theoretically be true, that the past is immutable. Over. Done. But what if it isn't? Doesn't May owe it to Marco and Pippa—yes, even Cristofana, not to mention the hundreds of thousands of strangers who might be saved by a simple Wikipedia printout or three—to try?

What does she have to lose that she hasn't already gambled with for curiosity's sake? May wouldn't be able to get her hands on actual antibiotics; procuring them would have been hard enough in the States, and like her, they'd come through ghosted anyway. But if she can find a doctor in Old Florence and explain about *Yersinia pestis* . . .

She's in no hurry to run into one of those freaky beaked men, but she leaves to fetch her laptop, returns, and logs into Google anyway, linking to Wiki and the printer, her fingers racing over the keys.

"You're working on your essays again?" Liam groans. "OK. Now I'm really freaked out."

"I know." She stands and looks him in the eye, relieved to find him looking back, really looking at her. May kisses him quickly on the forehead, unable or unwilling to explain. "Me too. But it'll be OK."

"Let me help you."

"I don't know how to."

"You've never known how, but seriously, we're going to talk about this. Tomorrow morning. About you. You say I don't know you, but I do. Pretty well, I think. Better than most. We'll go out to breakfast, just us, and you're gonna tell me everything that's happening to you, really happening, and I promise to try to believe you. I promise we'll make a plan. OK?"

She nods, eyes downcast.

"I've got to run those CDs I picked up over to Gwen at the library. Don't go anywhere," he insists, watching her too intently. "Better yet, why don't you come with?"

"No, I'm good," she says, shaking her head.

"Don't stay here alone. Please. You look like a ghost."

The words chill her . . . and fuel her determination. "Not me, dude. I'm a real, full-figured girl."

Li's crooked smile is the best reason in the world to stay—or to make it back, if it comes to that.

At dinner he doesn't take his eyes off her. Whenever May looks up at him over her microwaved linguini, she has to look away again.

She wants to let him help her, and *Liam could*, she thinks. If anyone can, it's Liam. But there's something hypnotic about what's happening to Cristofana — how whatever it is that was less than good in her before is growing bigger and meaner and more focused by the minute.

Long after Gwen turns in for the night, as Li's hauling himself off the couch to head to bed, May grabs his arm and pulls him back. She rests her hands tentatively on his shoulders. His neck glints sticky in the heat, soaking the edge of his T-shirt, and she pulls him close in a kiss that goes deep way too quickly. He bends her back against the cushions, but when May stiffens under his weight, he pulls back on his own, lifting her hands from his freckled neck, kissing one palm and slapping it away with a smile. "Nah, I'm not that cheap a date. This movie sucks. See you in the morning?" He stands with a groan, his voice softer, serious. "Breakfast?"

Their eyes meet, his shining in the blue TV light, and May nods, watching him disappear down the unlit hall and mouthing, "Thanks," into the dark.

Time Will Be Tricked

That night, she dreams she's dying, writhing, her body covered in lumps and sores.

It's almost dawn, and in the faint light, the creature at the end of her hotel-style bed, the bed she's just started sleeping in again, is familiar. It wears her face, but it's a winged, translucent thing made of light, chanting under its breath.

May doesn't believe in God, or devils, or angels, didn't, at least, before Florence, but she hurts, everything hurts, and the question forms itself. "Are you Death?"

The figure in odd garments — feathers, lace, and rags, wings hidden in the squirming hump on its back — nods. *Wake up now,* it urges. *Walk with me.*

No.

It's time.

No.

It's time now.

Some cogent part of May, the part that understands safe zones and that death has borders, lies heavy in sweat-soaked sheets; the other part craves relief, attainment, a sinking into the soft of knowledge. *I'm coming,* that part whispers in the dream, rising in sleep, swiveling to rest feet on the floor, sliding them mechanically into flip-flops to follow the winged shadow with its familiar walk, a sashay. The giggling child clings to its back like a flying monkey from *The Wizard of Oz,* peeking out from a moth-eaten wool blanket. *Coming.*

The moment the single, united form enters the portal — with dream May at its heels — May hears it, a wailing baby, and the sound holds the end of night like an egg in its palm. It rakes her brain like blades, and there are no slamming doors or searching voices. No reassuring sirens. No noise of rescue. Only a lone, intermittent cry of pain and outrage that echoes everywhere.

She finds herself in the familiar alley in Old Florence

in nothing but the long white T-shirt she slept in. On the ground by her feet, in a basket lined with straw, is Pippa, plump and red faced, writhing over the great play wings Cristofana must have fashioned for her out of wire and who knows what. The wings are crushed under her, and May watches a single feather float down, rocking on the still air. She can't say whether it's the feather or the act of looking up into May's face that calms her, but the big, dopey baby goes quiet. She offers a grasping hand, and May kneels, reaching back.

The touch is tickling and soft and stuns her, like being closed in a dark room, like the *clank* of a lock.

She never even felt the shock of her own flesh, but it's obvious now that Cristofana has dumped the baby at the exit and ducked back into the portal, leaving May stranded on the other side.

May straightens and juts out her dream arms—and they're hers, tan and freckled. She looks at her dream feet—sage rubber flip-flops, bony toes, mango nail polish. The panic hits hard, wave after wave of it. What did she expect? May turns and turns, her eyes scanning the predawn light of the alley, landing again on what Cristofana has left her, a whimpering baby in a basket.

She won't be back.

May thinks to leap into the portal after her twin,

hound her to Hell and back if she has to — haunt her, like the ghost May knows she'll become the moment she follows into the future — but she can't leave this baby exposed and alone in this deserted corner of the city. Cristofana knew she couldn't, and just before May wakes with a start, she imagines her twin on the other side, wielding her mojo, locking time's door forever.

May fumbles for her bedside lamp, breathing relief as light floods the room, her own room in the apartment in Florence Present, with Liam right behind the wall, asleep on the other side.

But the room and the night feel curiously hushed and hollow, and the looming emptiness of the portal accusing.

Keep your head.

Trying to ignore the paradox of how she is close to — and yet very far from — Marco . . . and her fear for the child Cristofana has in her clutches . . . and to what tonight's dream suggests about her mental state . . . May glances over at the Wikipedia printouts on her dresser: *The Black Death*, Yersinia pestis (*also/previously known as* Pasteurella pestis), *Plague* (Pathology, History, and Treatment), and *Plague Vaccine* (Streptomycin, Chloramphenicol, and Tetracycline), together with a printout on antibiotics generally, since no one then would know what the heck they were.

Keep your head.

She bolts upright, swinging out of bed and swiping the documents from the desk. True, Wiki isn't some peer-reviewed medical journal, but there has to be enough information there, presented simply, to help doctors of the day make sense of what they're up against. May has the opportunity to change everything, go back and bring the key to a cure with her, and maybe then they'll all be safe, Marco and Pippa, Cristofana, those countless doomed strangers. She slips into her flip-flops. The anxiety of the dream has made her decision feel all the more inevitable, but she'll go on her own terms, not Cristofana's. May won't be tricked or led. She'll get in and out of the past before her twin knows she's there, knows to steal her life and annihilate her.

As in the dream, May doesn't bother changing. It's the dark before dawn in Old Florence, as here, and she won't stick around, just long enough to traffic some information (and say good-bye . . . touch him once and say good-bye?). If she looks outrageous and alien, it will help them believe she is who she says she is, a girl from the future bearing strange gifts.

But who best to receive? The convent is the obvious choice, or the only one, and May hits the ground running, going ghost with the familiar surge of nausea, forgetting that she doesn't have to worry about her flip-flops slapping noisily on cobbles. In fact, because they slow her down, she takes them off, hooking them on her forefinger, dodging manure patties and other debris.

The dark crush of towers looms over her, but May finds the moon between the maze of buildings, fat and full, and its light soothes her. She more or less remembers the way south to the hills and the convent, though it hurts in a way to have Marco so close and not go to him. But May has to do this. Marietta speaks both English and Italian. She'll be able to read the printouts. She'll know powerful men in the Church who might direct things. What's more, she'll take one look at her sister's ghost double and know that something real and miraculous is happening. Identical though they appear, May isn't Cristofana. Her sister will also see that, and embrace the truth; she'll have to.

Despite her shaky confidence, May gets turned around, disoriented, comparing her mental map of the old city with the new. Her detour leads her onto a street where a hospital stood in Cristofana's day. May remembers passing this way on one of her twin's bleak tours, and it was bad enough the first time. Under cover of near darkness — it's not quite dawn — there seems to be a surplus of hushed, furtive activity out front. The only sounds are the creaking of rope pulleys as bodies are lowered from windows on planks into the extended arms of men on the ground, or the blunt thumping as they're hurled onto waiting carts. That, and the stamping of horses, swishing their tails at flies.

May remembers reading that even before the Great Mortality, Italian hospitals were the pride of all Europe. Often designed by famous architects and beautiful for it, they could boast careful attendants, clean linens, and learned physicians when a lot of medieval European hospitals couldn't. During the Black Death, some were spitting out five hundred bodies a day for burial. Besides giving medical care, they were retirement homes for old people, shelters for the homeless, and traveler way stations. More fodder for contagion.

Paused out of view, May takes her moment to hurry past the open entrance, glimpsing wavery figures in the torchlight inside, patients curled on temporary cots or propped against walls and pillars, the crisscrossing shadows of attending nuns. An indignant stray rooster shoots out the doorway, clucking, driven from underfoot, and May pauses again for just an instant, wondering if she should just go the direct route.

But even if she weren't ghosted, in this getup—flip-flops, arms and legs exposed—with her lousy Italian, they'd think she was a deranged prostitute, or just deranged, and shut her away. No. May needs a buffer, a translator.

She keeps going, trying to drown out Cristofana's voice in her head. *Time will be tricked but never cheated.*

Dodging a cartload departing for the churchyard, May looks for a gap between buildings and makes for the river and the bridge. Once she has them in view, she rights her course. The sun is rising beyond the hills, and by the time she makes it through the nearest city gate and across the still Arno, dawn light falls softly on a summer landscape streaked with dew.

Swallows dive-bomb the golden grass for insects, bringing May a moment's peace, a stubborn hope, and by the time she reaches the arched convent doorway scarred with a red X, she's as calm and ready as she knows how to be.

She reaches pointlessly for the knocker, but the stooped woman who answered the last time, when Cristofana rapped, appears as if on cue, tiny in the massive doorway with her broom. She points to the X, waving May away, then thinks better of it, setting her broom aside, her expression tender and sorrowful. She must think May is Cristofana.

"Suor Arcangela?" May asks.

The woman winces, shaking her head, her eyes full of pity and grief. "No, *mia cara. È troppo tardi.*" She opens the huge door, gesturing inside. Even in the curtained gloom May can see that the simple, stark furniture in the long hall has been covered with sheets. The cots are cleared out. The splintered floor is swept clean. The silence is vast, and May backs away from it, her ghost hands eluding the woman's grasp.

For a moment, it's hard to know who she is, hard to feel a border between herself and Cristofana. Suddenly the dream makes sense. Cristofana's one solid link to her past, her life in the past, has been severed. She has no reason to stay now, apart from Marco and Pippa, whom she's only known as long as May has.

Hurrying out through the gate in the hedges, May almost trips (mentally, at least) over a man in a long robe, a priest maybe—no, a doctor; May saw the same costume on the beaked men in the aisles of the hospital the time Cristofana brought her by. His robe is tangled around his legs, which are bent under him at an obscene angle, like a very frail old man's. May knows that many of his fellow physicians fled for the hills at the first signs that spring. This man must have stayed, administering to the dying, sacrificing for them, and his herbs and poultices and urine treatments proved as useless for him as for his patients, and now that he's dying, he's come looking for God.

Hands shaking, frantic now—she has to get back

to the portal before a grieving, enraged-at-God-and-the-universe Cristofana learns she's here — May blindly fishes the ghost pages out of her ghost backpack and waves them in his face, trying to get his attention before it's too late, stammering in horrible Italian. *Help . . . another . . . smart . . . doctor . . . where?* But he's ranting even louder, and anyway, May has gone limp, her hand sinking to her side. Because the ink on the pages, she sees with despair, like every other dark or defining edge on her and her belongings, has been ghosted. Against the barely opaque paper, the pages might as well be blank.

She's found the resolve to back away when she feels that now-familiar rush of nausea, that hollow reeling, together with the jarring sensation of the doctor's hands clamping on to one of her ankles.

Trapped in the heat and stink and contagion of *here,* May tries to pull free, but the man is looking up at her as if his life depends on it; he has very little life left to speak of. He's sickly pale and breathing funny. His eyes are wild.

Thrusting his free fist at her like a boxer, he cries out something in Italian that she can't understand.

"*Per favore* —" *Just, please, take your hands away. . . .*

He doesn't seem to hear, murmuring, "*Caterina, amore mio, sono pronto,*" and he looks at her with something like love, demented, mistaking her for someone, his breath heaving now. It occurs to May that she must have looked like a proper ghost to him, one that suddenly, before his eyes, became flesh. *Flesh. Real. Here.*

Now he extends both hands—how do you refuse the dying?—releasing her ankle but lunging for her nearest hand. He's incredibly quick and strong, considering. *Please, don't . . . don't touch. . . .*

He has her hand in a hot clamp, her knuckles crushed, and she feels hysterical but can't get away. In that instant, crayon-flat faces, comically distorted—the faces of everyone she loves—flip through her thoughts like the pages in a child's hand-drawn book. Her mom and dad, Gwen, Sarah, True, Liam . . . Marco? "*È vero, amore mio.*"

The hand that felt so warm at her ankle now burns like ice. The strength drains from his frail grip, and he kisses her bruising knuckles, one by one, tenderly, his lips cracked and faintly blue, and May feels it in every cell, atom, and molecule of her body. She feels it all. He slumps forward until his head knocks the ground and her hand slides free.

"Please," she tries, lifting his head or trying, her skin cringing on contact, but when she manages to turn his face to her, May has nothing to say. What can she possibly say? His eyes are blank. This is the first person taken by plague that has actually *been* a person for her, not a corpse or an abstraction but a live person robbed of life. Her backpack slides off, still ghosted like the printouts fluttering nearby on the ground. They must not have corresponded with whatever Cristofana brought into the future. As a page tumbles away in a breeze, May feels the sting of tears.

Her mind sifts through a thousand emotions. Pity, sorrow, and—like a kick to the chest—a fear that knocks her to her knees beside a very contagious corpse.

If her life wasn't over before, it very likely is now.

Strega

There is only one place she can think to go, not that she's thinking straight. Driven by panic, May hurries past the few incredulous early-morning strangers who spot her en route to the bridge. Once through the city gate, out of the open, May can dodge from alley to alley or otherwise conceal herself and her strange (highly revealing, by fourteenth-century standards) clothing.

In the long alley beside the workshop, which cuts back to a claustrophobic fenced-in garden, she slips off her bracelets, stashing them and her flip-flops under an upturned terra-cotta window box. She pads to the front entrance, rapping softly with a knuckle, though the display awning has been taken down and the street-facing window shuttered. *Where are you?*

Her waiting heart hammers, and when no one comes, she tries the door, terrified.

You can't be dead. You can't be.

The space has changed radically since May was here last. It's dim and dusty inside, cluttered as ever, but now evidence of Cristofana's scavenging is everywhere. *She's like a raven,* May thinks, feeling wired and alert, circling the silent room, trying not to hate her twin and failing.

There are the shiny things, of course, what Cristofana steals outright from the deserted homes of wealthy merchants taken by plague: candlesticks with beeswax tapers, jeweled rings, an ornate dagger. There's a Venetian glass mirror with a chipped gilt frame, a now-soiled oriental carpet, pewter plates and pitchers.

Looking more closely, as early daylight begins to spill in from the one high window that isn't shuttered, she sees an unfamiliar—and gigantic—carved bed with a feather mattress, hung with rich curtains. Cristofana must have dismantled and transported it piece by piece, or bewitched an army of children into scurrying through the streets, hunched under their burden, in the dead of the night. As big as a barge, the bed takes up a quarter of the large studio space, and May's tempted to run a hand over its rumpled silk coverlet and imagine Marco lying there, but then, it seems, she'll have to imagine Cristofana beside him. If anything's clear, agonizingly, it's that Cristofana has taken things a step further with Marco. She's moved in.

The stolen finery has no natural place in the jumble of easels and half-carved statues, paint pots and skinny chickens, silk and straw, but even stranger and more incongruous is the evidence strewn about of Cristofana's own enigmatic craft: delicate eggshells still sticky with inner membrane, bird feathers and shells, bunches of dried herbs hanging, the dainty skeleton of a dead bird, owl pellets. These objects, together with the baskets of pewter flatware and tarnished jewels, tell of a feral, singsongy creature, and the desk in the corner where the master's business was conducted is crowded with vials and beakers. "*Strega*," she had called herself, and yes, when May consulted one of the dictionaries at the apartment, she understood. *Strega*. Witch.

Even odder than that barge of a stolen bed, that carved monstrosity, is what has to be the baby's bed, a giant round market basket overflowing with feathers, as if someone had sliced open a dozen pillows and poured their contents inside.

It looks itchy, but May can see that someone has carefully culled through and left only the small downy under feathers, the soft ones, May knows.

Pippa is loved. But by whom?

Does Cristofana leave the baby completely in Marco's care? Dump her there while she traipses about raiding dead people's houses and murdering kittens and bullying nuns? What are they to each other? And does he even know that May and Cristofana are two different people? If not, what must he think of her? He can only have deduced that "she" is crazy and learned to live with it, the way he's learned to live daily with death and deserted streets and the anguished moaning beyond his walls at night.

Remembering, May roots quickly through the wardrobe, extracting one of Cristofana's crazy stolen dresses, the simplest, though also — and here May surrenders to a moment's vanity or hope — bright red and fitted at the waist, with a low-curving embroidered front. She has to lift the hem when she walks, but no use alarming Marco any more than she has to. She stuffs her white sleep T and Old Navy bikini briefs, the last telltale artifacts, beneath a pile of linens in a basket.

How have they been surviving? How will any of them survive now that Cristofana's abandoned them? Struck by her isolation, May feels like an interloper, a spy in their home—and what are they, some kind of family now? That's how it looks. Except that Surrogate Mom has bailed ship and left a changeling in her place, one with absolutely no survival skills, one too sad and overwhelmed by good-byes unsaid to know which end is up.

Light-headed with exhaustion, May lies down, hiking the scarlet gown over her knees, sinking into the soft feather mattress. She takes in the already familiar room with bleary eyes (thinking how quickly a place can begin to look like "home," or, for that matter, stop looking like one).

The effort of trying to block out mental images of Cristofana lurking in the dream, dark at the foot of her bed, of Pippa, filthy and feathered and drooping over her guardian's shoulder, sucking her thumb, of Marco off somewhere, gaunt with worry, his eyes bruised and sunken, his sketch board blank, keeps her awake for a time. But in minutes, May is sound asleep.

Why

May wakes an hour or two later — the light is bright and stark — with Marco and Pippa still nowhere to be seen. Daylight has her on her feet in an instant. *Jesus!* She shouldn't be here, not after the doctor. *Did you come here to save them, or kill them?* She shouldn't be sleeping in their beds and touching their things.

So May grabs a crust of bread from the table and spends what must be the next twenty-four hours hugging her knees in the alley beside the workshop.

Even as it starts to get dark again, and the harsh cries and drunken singing of men entering and exiting the tavern a few doorways down ring through the streets, she resists going in to Marco. If she's caught plague, she'll infect him and the baby. May stares into space, willing herself away from the present. Even if she fled to the remote alley with its faintly scrawled symbol, the portal would be gone, she knows, dismantled, and if it isn't, she couldn't enter now anyway. Her life no longer belongs to her. Not for the next few days, at least. By then she'll know if she's marked or not, if that life is over.

May can't muster an opinion—about this or anything. An emotion. Hope. Regret. Not even hunger. She might as well be in ghost form again, except that she isn't, and at regular intervals May pushes her long, loose sleeve off her shoulder to check for sores in the soft crescent of her armpit, waiting for fever and sweat and black blotches. But nothing comes.

Nothing but the night again. By daylight, the alley isn't worth remarking on. It's not dirty, not clean, just damp and blank, a storage place for the stonemason next door. At night, though, it fills with sound, men carousing in the distance, yes, but also nonhuman snuffling and scratching, and May knows she isn't alone here, that other travelers with teeth and tails pass this way to and from the garden. She huddles in her harlot's gown, and waiting becomes her occupation.

May settles in a hollow inside herself, like a hibernating animal, suspended in space and time. She isn't sure how many hours pass before her dry mouth and the dull ache in her head inform her that she needs to get up and find food, find water.

Before sunrise, she sneaks into the kitchen garden behind the workshop and picks cherry tomatoes from a vine, stuffing them into her mouth, juice and seeds spilling everywhere. They're delicious. She licks dewy leaves until Pippa's voice, the contented noise of a small child waking before the adults and talking back to her imaginary world, rivets her. May darts out of the garden and back to her grim hideout until Pippa's happy shouts sound out front, and the pull of life proves too strong.

May watches from around the corner as they head out for the morning, deciding it won't hurt to tag along. As long as she keeps hidden, keeps her distance. If she's going to die, she'll do it in the fresh air, with a view.

Marco carries a long, curved basket, probably some kind of fish or eel net, and heads straight for the southern edge of the city, walking a mile or two along a cart road running parallel to the river, past the bridges, till the sloping wall of buildings that crowd the Arno's shoreline thin and taper out. With nowhere to hide in the wide open, May finally has to let them go on without her. She conceals herself beside a stashed rowboat flipped on its side. Stretched in the trodden grass, listening to the pull of the river, she feels exhaustion in every limb. Though it's the last thing she means to do, she falls asleep again, and when she wakes, Pippa is beside her, weaving wildflowers into her hair.

Am I dreaming?

May sits up, inching away on her backside, her eyes wide on Marco behind the child. He has hollow circles under his eyes, a pallor below his caramel skin, and he looks terrible . . . and beautiful . . . and terrible. May fights the urge to stand and touch his face. *I can do it now,* she thinks—remembering her overwhelming urge to reach out to him the day she stood behind his easel at the workshop—*I can touch you.*

And then she thinks of her own response, when the dying doctor reached for her. *Don't don't don't touch. . . .*

Pippa's after a frog hopping along the shore, so May reaches and dips her finger in the river mud. She scrawls an X over the exposed hollow of her throat, speaking with her eyes, and when Marco tries to reach for her, pulls away fiercely. He sets his basket aside, his amber eyes hard to read, and before he can use them to convince her to stay, she gets up and strides off. She walks until she finds the strength to run, the sides of her gown bunched in her fists, and runs until, looking back, she can't see them anymore.

But they're all she has, so a bewildered May lurks in wait, learning to look and not be seen, watching from some hiding place or another till they pass. They've made a game out of finding frogs. Obviously distracted, Marco still takes the time to lay down his basket and fit a frog into Pippa's pudgy hands, where it slides out again, a leaping complaint—and then he finds her another, his dark eyes as fixed and patient as a heron's.

Pippa seems to have shot up overnight, become a toddler. The little girl manages a few steps and then topples over, whimpering showily until he plucks her up and dusts her off. That or she struggles upright again, soldiering on, oblivious and determined. Marco is neither gentle nor impatient with her . . . only present . . . attentive when he has to be. Mainly he lets her go about her business until the water or other trouble attracts her. They have a quiet, easy rapport, but there's something too measured about his movements, as if his very life depends on the ability to concentrate. May can only imagine how confused he is, and she's confused, too, not knowing what sort of presence Cristofana has become in their lives, what impact she's had. Her domestic sprawl in the workshop certainly suggests that she's wormed her way into their world completely.

They thought I was her.

Pippa falls again, twisting in the effort to get vertical, and looks right up the hill at May, her smile confirming everything. May ducks out of view until they set off again, then follows from a reasonable distance.

Marco never notices her, or at least he acts like he doesn't, though Pippa often does and laughs and babbles. It's a game to her. Hide-and-seek.

May follows through the winding streets and alleys as the pair meanders—Marco sometimes taking up Pippa's hand, sometimes riding her on his shoulders, and when at last they reach the workshop, Marco hustles Pippa inside and bolts the door behind them. May stands paralyzed—the last thing she wants is to return to the stony gloom of the alley, but it hasn't been long enough yet, not quite.

The front shutters open, startling her, and when he spots her there, his expression is intense, if no more readable than before. The door swings open, though he doesn't emerge, and the unlit interior of the workshop looks forbidding from the walkway, where the sun now shines hard on stone and stucco.

When he doesn't emerge or wave her in, May steps to

the doorway and, with halting Italian and pantomime, explains that she'll isolate herself in the garden for a couple more days and that he and Pippa must keep away. He nods gravely, and after she settles in, he opens the garden door and sets down a blanket, a steaming bowl of lentils, a crust of bread, and a cup of wine.

May isn't sure how long she stays out there, with this feeding ritual repeated at intervals.

She sleeps and dreams and sweats, and is afraid of sweating, afraid of the tiniest headache, of the bug bites she mistakes as buboes. Luckily the weather holds out, and in the end it's only the insects that plague her. May spends her nights swaddled in the blanket to ward them off, heat or no heat, and the wool smells like what has to be Marco, and it's a good, strong smell that keeps her mind on life.

When she's certain that enough time has elapsed, that she isn't contagious, May stands up, uncertain about everything else. She waits for him to notice her out there, for his awareness to shift to her, for permission, and he opens the door almost immediately, waving her in.

His silence is ominous. May's eyes are still adjusting to the dim when she spots Pippa hanging over the edge of the big barge of a bed, pulling the silk coverlet and a sea of clothes and cloaks off in a landslide that takes her with it. Hitting the floor with the rest of the pile, the toddler starts to wail.

Marco hauls baby and bedclothes off the floor, holding her and rocking her almost maniacally; he's been left with this, a child, and must be confused, resentful, but he seems less overwhelmed than tired.

May almost wishes she were a ghost again, safe from hard edges, from the confusion Cristofana has left them in. Pippa's savage cries tempt her forward—May wants to help, make it stop—but she's frozen to the spot.

When the cries cease, Marco nestles Pippa in the big bed again, gating her in with a rolled blanket like a pro. He turns with a weary sigh, an air of familiarity as if to say, *You deal with it*, as if May were in fact a young mother and he the stay-at-home dad who's reached his limit. This is not a sensation she's ready to have, and it seems to May, somewhat irrationally, that Cristofana has kept her promise. She has ruined everything.

I will take his smile forever, in your honor, and he will think all along it was you.

What else would Marco think? She and Cristofana are one and the same to him, and there's no telling what horrors or humiliations he's suffered on her watch.

May can't look at him. She doesn't dare. For all she

knows, he hates her now or thinks she's a monster. Would he even look at her again the way he did the day he mended her knee? What if the man she saw looking out at her through laughing amber eyes that day no longer exists — destroyed by the plague, or Cristofana, or both?

Even Pippa doesn't laugh or babble when May approaches her now. She rolls away with her thumb in her mouth, her forehead sweaty, her feet and knees filthy from that morning's outing. The thumb doesn't soothe her, and in no time she's wailing again, belly down, kicking her feet with a dull thump on the mattress, pitiful and inconsolable. She's obviously hungry, but May has no idea what they've been feeding her. She feels useless, horrible, but Marco has already mashed up a dish of what looks like fruit with porridge. *Good,* May thinks, *no wet nurse need apply,* relieved that Pippa can manage hard food.

The little girl eats with a pout on her face, squinting at her surrogate father until he scowls back playfully. After she's had her fill, Pippa collapses over her pile of covers and capes, sucking her thumb until the hand falls away in sleep.

Then things get really awkward.

Marco just sits there, watching May from his chair. He can't seem to decide whether he loves her or hates her. Sometimes his amber eyes pierce in a way that makes her aware of every inch of her body. Sometimes he clamps them closed as if he can't stand the sight of her. *Thanks, Cristofana,* thinks May, not knowing what to address first.

She has memorized the words for *I'm sorry* but doesn't speak them. He doesn't speak, either, but when finally May looks at him as directly as she can, she feels his eyes warm to her, feels him watching her even after she looks away.

He gets up, walks to the front display window, and folds the inside shutters closed. He crosses back to her with that alarming look on his face, then eases her back against the wall. It might be anything, that look, and it's a little of everything: lust, pleading, accusation, anger . . . definitely exhaustion. He smells rank and rich, and it dizzies her. May read somewhere in Gwen's heaps of museum and gallery materials that medieval people rarely bathed. They carried around carved apples full of herbs and spices, or dried posies, to trick their noses and distract from the stench everywhere. She can't be smelling too good herself at this point. He has her pinned, and when he kisses her, deep and hard, with a familiarity that frightens and excites her, May knows for sure that he has this all wrong. He thinks she's Cristofana. In May's absence, some kind of twisted intimacy has obviously developed between them, because he seems as likely to strangle as to keep kissing this lunatic girl who went away and left him with a child.

At the moment, May doesn't care if she isn't that girl. She can't help it. She kisses him back, and back and back.

Later, she'll make Marco understand what he's been dealing with, who he's been dealing with, and who he hasn't.

But for now he's longed for her, and he's angry, and it's all her fault. *All my fault*, thinks May irrationally, confused by her own willingness to go along, to let him believe whatever he wants, believe anything if she can own his sigh of resignation and his mouth moving over hers, and the pressure of his hands, the way he breathes her in and takes her breath. If it lets her keep this lonely, beautiful stranger for herself—keep him close, needing her—then she'll be anyone, for a while, even Cristofana.

He's so intense she doesn't know what to do . . . until she does. The sleeping child has the bed, so they kneel together in a crouch, settling on the floor among coils of rope and oily stains and splinters and sawdust and chicken feathers.

It's hard to look at him as he eases her down, his

eyes urgent and sorrowful while he undresses and lowers himself over, pulling her middle close in rough, paint-smeared hands, smoothing the sides of her crimson gown up. So she meets the blank stare of an unfinished sculpture beyond them, until at last he starts kissing her again, and she kisses back, a little fiercely, rolling on top of him in a bliss of rising away and falling and sliding and biting her lip as he moves inside her, moves and moves, and it's like reeling or flying apart.

May wakes later on splintery hardwood, tucked into the same wool blanket she had outside, like a mummy in her bandages. It's sticky hot because he's sealed her in on every side, sweetly, thoughtfully, and now he sits in a chair in a corner, eating an apple. With Pippa wide awake and prancing first in her big bird's nest, blowing feathers off pudgy palms, and then on the bed, he's been watching May sleep. There is nothing quite like being looked at that way by an artist.

May feels sore and ripe and real and wonders did she really lose her virginity with . . . what? A man who no longer exists? An afterimage? How could something that physical not be real? She isn't sorry or disappointed, not at all, but there's something bittersweet because of Liam. She wouldn't change anything, May thinks, meeting Marco's dark eyes, wouldn't give this back or undo it, but part of her feels like a thief.

He takes another bite of the apple, green and bruised, his gaze intent on her. He is too beautiful for words.

Good thing, because she doesn't have any.

May rises slowly, adjusting her mangled gown. She folds the blanket, sets it aside, and tidies up a little. Like a visitor. Because in the end she's just a visitor, isn't she? A traveler. No matter what Cristofana thinks.

Time will be tricked but never cheated.

All this suspect activity visibly alarms Marco, who relaxes only when she leads him to the bed. They lie beside Pippa, and May sleeps like Pippa in the heat of Marco's arms, which tighten around them in the night whenever one or the other tosses and turns. Later, he wakes again to find her by the window. May lets him blot away her tears with his thumbs, and his own eyes are so worried, so haunted, she strains for words. "I won't leave you," she says.

It's the best lie she can think of—*can't* and *won't* not being the same thing—and she lets him lead her back to bed. They lie a long time in silence, face-to-face in the moonlight with Pippa behind them, before he says anything.

Marco doesn't talk much, as a rule, and doesn't

seem concerned that she doesn't, either. But now he asks, "*Perché?*" hoarsely, almost mournfully, running his fingers along the edge of her face.

Why?

Why what?

Why would she come back? Or why would she leave him?

Such a big little word, *why*.

A Simple, Closed World

Once she's positive she hasn't infected them, when they, too, exhibit no signs of plague, May relaxes into the uneasy rhythms of the household.

Marco wakes first, rousing Pippa before dawn to fish and hunt frogs by the river. He always seems surprised when May elects to go along, which suggests that Cristofana didn't. He seems surprised by many things, with good reason, and over the course of a day, May often looks up and finds him watching her, puzzling. Her Italian is so halting that she's more or less stopped talking voluntarily. If he speaks, she does her best to answer, but sometimes she just stares back blankly, mute and sorry.

When the river fog burns off, the trio heads back to pick over scant goods in various black-market haunts in the neighborhood, weed around the salad greens, herbs, and tomatoes in the kitchen garden, or, while Pippa naps, manage the dormant workshop.

Through a mostly wordless shorthand system they've developed, talking with their eyes and their hands, Marco teaches her to grind pigment for paint and help sort his sprawl of correspondence, cracked parchments, old marble orders, and shipping documents, all more or less by appearance. What she can't explain is that she took Italian her sophomore year of high school and reads the language way better than she speaks it, so some documents are of real interest.

Not long before the Great Mortality ravaged Florence — she learns in letters from his father and brother addressed from a village near Orvieto — Marco was admitted into the guild, the Company of Saint Luke, meaning that one day he'll open an independent workshop and become his own master, with his own powerful patron.

Thanks to Gwen, May knows that even when he sets up shop for himself, Marco won't be free to paint the images that seem to crowd his mind and scream for color. Like his late master, an early plague victim, Marco will have a wealthy patron who chooses his subjects and influences his style and the way he works. Most commissions will have religious themes, and the patron will flatter and insert himself into every allegory and heroic pose, whether the artist wants him there or not.

Marco's shop, like this one—which will pass to his master's heirs once the plague is sorted out—will probably be on the ground floor of a city-center building, a simple shop that could as easily be a shoemaker's or a butcher's. It will throng with boarders, apprentices, and assistants, and churn out suits of armor, theatrical costumes, and tombstones as well as sculpture and altarpieces, keeping enough chickens underfoot to feed everyone and provide eggs for tempera to bind the pigments for paint.

In an unsent letter to his brother, Marco complains (though May's translation is painful):

> *There will be the boys and the chickens and noise always, and I will never know again that blessed silence I knew as a youth in Father's barn, when my thoughts and pictures were my own, when the urge to create filled me every morning like breath*

> *and rose again in my thoughts at night, after the day's labors, like the moon.*

In another, earlier letter, also unsent, Marco wrote of there being no one left alive in a certain church to check his fresco work:

> *The sole remaining priest fled some days ago with the altar gold to his nephew's country villa. He instructs from afar, but Master leaves this work to me and the other apprentices, convinced he won't be paid for the commission. As of yesterday, he is confined to his bed, like our parents before him, and shouts visitors away from his door.*
>
> *I confess I feel each day more like a fatherless son, a motherless child, a man of the ruined world. You say I am free, not bound to Sire's fallow land, but freedom is a vast emptiness, like God . . . a speaking wind.*

In the afternoon, until the light dies, Marco paints—sometimes on a canvas, but more often right on the rear plaster wall of the workshop, fresco-style—and May knows enough to stay invisible, though he never asks her to. Even Pippa seems to get it, content to play in the garden with Cristofana's stash of stolen cards and dice games, tops and balls. There's even a wooden sword out there, a paint-chipped hobbyhorse.

Marco works tirelessly, obsessively, stretching his aching arm. He'll start with a formal outline on paper — today another Madonna and Child, drawn and pricked through with hundreds of tiny painstaking holes. He fixes the paper to the wall, shakes charcoal dust over, and paints the form beneath the page. Only he doesn't, really.

Today the outline of loving arms extended, the mother's secret smile, the infant, plump and assured, morph into a grinning, implacable skeleton, Death on a gaunt horse, reaching down for a child, robbing a mother of hope.

"I will paint it over," he tells her later in Italian, with a sigh of what can only be regret, because in his apologetic view, the work is good — like the sprawling nude and the demon in chains the days before — very good. His best yet. "Tomorrow. I will try again." He says it as if this is what she needs to hear, what she deserves.

At night they sleep in a sweaty tangle, all three, and this dark man kisses their foreheads while they dream.

There is something so deceptively simple in all this,

so natural and domestic, that May almost forgets that she's been robbed.

She almost lets herself fall head over heels in love with Marco, with Pippa, with the early-morning fishing excursions, and the smell of rosemary in the little crowded city garden, and the act of kneading bread dough made from scratch, from grain, baking it in an oven that's no more than a hole in the wall. With all of it.

She almost forgets about Liam, and Gwen, and her parents, and True, and her friends, and her dreams. What recalls her, what brings her back every afternoon when the sun starts to set, when Pippa starts whimpering because she's wet herself or wants dinner, are Marco's daily paintings, so startling and wrong in a such a simple, closed world.

A few days later, when May is walking home from a failed search for produce, it occurs to her to detour and check on the portal. It's a long shot—Cristofana wouldn't have left it open—but on the other hand, May poses no threat in ghost form, which is what she'll assume the moment she crosses over. She can't usurp Cristofana in the future or force her twin back into the portal and the past. May can't right the balance now. Only Cristofana can, and her twin knows that.

But some part of Cristofana, May supposes, must worry that if she severs the link from the future, the old rules will no longer apply, that she won't be able to restore travel if and when she decides it's time. Would her magic hold hundreds of years away? May would certainly worry along those lines, but then again, May is as ignorant as she is cautious. Can it really be that simple to manipulate the space-time continuum, or whatever the hell her twin is doing? Maybe magic is that simple. A ring, a poppet, an incantation or two, but May can't credit it. Her mind doesn't work that way, though Cristofana's clearly does. Maybe they're two parts of the same puzzle, mirror halves of a single mind.

She can't believe it hasn't dawned on her to check before—with her (portion of?) mind too much on Marco and finding food and staying out of the path of the plague—but it's got to be worth a try, and May feels her step quicken as she heads south toward the alley where the sideways 8 is scrawled.

Ducking in, May gropes the air, and sure enough, it's there, still there, that formless absence with its mild magnetic pull. To test, May thrusts a tingling hand through but pulls it back, panicked by a surge of conflicting feelings. What will she find on the other side? What has Cristofana been up to in May's name? What if her twin dismantles the portal with May on the other side? If Cristofana catches her out in ghost shape, in the future, will that be it? And what if May does find a way to reverse all this — and never sees Marco and Pippa again?

But she does step through, tentatively at first, though the sensation of intense atomic movement is so swift and jarring that the passage is over before she knows it. May finds herself standing in her bedroom in Florence Present, a ghost furiously faced with a girl, her flesh double stretched long across the bed in one of Gwen's silky nightgowns with *Vogue* open on her lap.

"A visitor!" Cristofana croons, her voice thick with irony. "How lovely."

"Are they home?" May whispers, gesturing as she floats forward.

"No . . . they are embarked on one of that woman's ceaseless errands. I have been sick in bed for days. It surprises me, frankly, that you have stayed away so long."

Like May, Cristofana has had to attend to Now, be present in her present and not consumed every second by what she's missing, by the disappearing days and hours of her rightful life, hasn't she? She can't have stayed in bed the whole time.

"And how are you enjoying my life?" May accuses,

stopping when she reaches the bed, her ghost legs merging with the end of the mattress.

"Much more than you did. I have no doubt."

May ignores the faint, wry smile and just glares back at her.

The waiting silence actually seems to unsettle Cristofana, who closes her magazine, if slowly, then smoothes it with her palm. "In truth"—she looks up—"it is exceedingly dull here, and I cannot sleep."

"Why's that, Cristofana? Bad conscience?"

"No, never. I simply find it too noisy. There is a forever of bleating and howling out there, like a monstrous wolf in the night."

"Sirens."

Cristofana looks up sharply. "What?"

"Never mind." May sighs. "It's a little early for bed, isn't it? Tell me what you've been doing."

"I told you. I have been deathly ill."

They stare at each other, exasperated.

"I'm sure you know now," Cristofana goes on, her tone shifting, "that our duck has terrors when she wakes. The infant cries out until someone comes to her."

"Not on my watch. But does this mean you miss her?" The ice in May's voice thaws. *Incredible*. "You do, don't you? You miss Pippa."

Cristofana nods. "It is my newest sin against myself. He called me once a mockery of motherhood but meant it not."

"And Marco. Do you miss Marco, too?"

Silence.

"Because I've been wanting to thank you. You were right, you know, about everything. He does taste like honey from the hills. . . ."

Silence.

"He *is* a master with his hands. . . ."

"I believe you once said, wisely . . . how do you say? . . . *Shut up, bitch*. . . ." Cristofana's smile has the violence of a lightning bolt.

"Hey, they're your words."

Pulling herself upright, her back straight against the padded headboard, Cristofana tilts forward, as with a secret. "But how long, *bella*, will it take him to see that you are not me? You couldn't be, could you?"

Silence.

"He calls me his pirate queen. If you would mimic me, you must bring him a new surprise every day: a spool of colored ribbon, the skull of a cat, a bottle of aged sherry, a tarnished spoon. Marco likes surprises. He tells me I am beautiful but mad, like a dream of perfection one day and a sleek harpy the next, a perverse and reckless shadow, and this you will never be. These you will never be. Though you may sleep through the night."

"I do. . . . I sleep in his arms."

"He told me on the last morning we spent together that I was the sound of his heart waking and breaking. Does he tell you such things?" She scoffs. "I think not."

"You're surprisingly sentimental for a sociopath, Cristofana. Has anyone ever told you that?"

"Mock me if you like. I do not know these words. But you don't know him."

And just like that, May doesn't.

She thinks of the way she has followed Marco with her eyes, day after day—for how many days now?—hungry for his hands on her. Marco hasn't touched her since that first time, except to hold her in the dark, except in forming the protective circle with Pippa while they sleep. He is always and feverishly working. What goes through his head is as much a mystery as his frightening paintings. Marco would be easy to love and hard to know, May thinks, and the language barrier is the least of it.

"I can't *sleep*," Cristofana complains loudly, jarring May out of her thoughts. "I can't I can't I can't." Her eyes, an exact replica of what May used to see in the mirror each morning—when she had a mirror—do in fact look drawn and puffy, raccoon ringed. May wonders if her own look as bad. She realizes, without admitting it aloud, that she hasn't been sleeping well, either, even in Marco's arms. *We correspond.*

"Then just come back home," May says feebly, "where you belong."

This weak appeal seems to rally Cristofana, who strikes a suggestive pose on the bed, all snaky in Gwen's silk nightgown. (*Who said you could wear that?*) "I cannot," she says, "Li-um would not part with me now. . . ."

"If you lay one hand on him . . ."

"You'll do what, traveler?"

"Look," May begins, pacing around the side of the bed. "You have what you want. Just be here and be satisfied you're not back there. You're not dead." May lifts her arms, as evidence. "But then again, in case you haven't noticed, neither am I."

"I cannot sleep," Cristofana complains again, softly now, sadly, glancing toward the window. "I cannot go out."

"Why not?"

"Because . . . it may please you to know . . . I am frightened. This is not my Florence. It is crowded and fast and terrible in its noise."

"Just come back."

Silence.

"Fine," May almost spits out. "Then be content. Appreciate what you've taken from me."

Her face darkens, remembering what drove her away, no doubt. "I cannot."

"Then what? What the fuck do you want from me?"

May isn't sure if she's being taken in, but Cristofana looks genuinely small and needy there on the hotel-style bed—so different than the vast barge they sleep on back at the workshop—and even helpless in her modern costume. "Tell me what to do . . . how to be here."

May longs to do something with her hands, her flesh—it's not often that Cristofana reveals vulnerability, and not being able to act on it makes May feel half mad with frustration, unmoored, as if she'll float away. "Try being nice," she says, "for one thing. Don't hurt anyone. We're all very nice in the future."

"Bah."

"Seriously. Are they OK? Is Liam OK?"

"I find your lover very amusing. . . ."

"It's not a finders-keepers kind of thing. You're aware of that, right?"

"Are you?"

"One day you'll answer a question with something other than a question."

“Keep them safe,” Cristofana says, opening her magazine again, settling back against the pillows as May—reassured but only just; formless but still, somehow, exhausted—turns back toward the only home she has left. “And I pledge the same.”

The Body Is a Curious Thing

May wakes the next night with her chest in a knot. As soon as her eyes adjust, she slips out from under Marco's arm and heads to the hearth, groping along the stone mantel for the tinderbox and a candle. She lights a waxy stub and slips out the garden door with it.

She sits under a new moon among the motionless plants. There isn't a breeze to be had, but the scent of rosemary and thyme and lavender still permeates the air. May looks up and can almost make out the Big Dipper, and the thrill of the familiar makes her eyes tear up.

It's been less than twenty-four hours, but now that she knows she can go back, even ghosted, the pull of the portal is irresistible, just as it was from the other side. It's as if the device and its options make it impossible to be happy or content in either place.

May returns inside but can't lie down again, can't do anything but glance with mounting sorrow at Marco and Pippa sleeping soundly. She can only pace and wonder, wonder and pace, understanding that somehow Cristofana is on the other side, wondering and pacing, living, like her, in both places, both times, and in neither.

May now bends to kiss them good night—or good-bye; she still isn't sure which—kisses as light as moths' wings, first on Pippa's temple and then Marco's. There is no time for second thoughts, but May has them anyway, fleeting ones. She doesn't belong here, doesn't belong with them, and Cristofana does. May just hopes that her twin will learn to deserve them.

Marco and Pippa.

She says each name softly under her breath as she makes for the alley, ducking and dodging through old, bleak streets under cover of darkness.

Tonight, when May comes through the portal, Cristofana is at the chair by the tall window, gazing forlornly out at the sliver of city visible through encroaching walls. May has never seen anyone look so sad, and because Cristofana is a sort of mirror, May feels it, too, that sadness. Or maybe she's been feeling it all along.

"Why don't you tell me what happened with your sister," she says softly, trying to be kind, to build a bridge between them. They are so alike, after all, but when Cristofana lifts her head, her look is startled, ferocious.

"Marietta?" May adds, wary now, on her guard. "At the convent? Did you get to see her again before . . . you left?"

She's still standing at the invisible mouth of the portal when Cristofana lunges, howling with rage and anguish, falling through, the wind of her body taking Ghost May with her.

They collide inside the portal with a crushing force, as if every bone in May's body is being mashed and mauled in a blender. It's pitch-dark in there, or she's blinded by pain, but May hears Cristofana's voice in her ear, in her mind—May can't be sure; it seems to echo all around and inside her—screaming, screaming like a wildcat, and all at once they are two bodies fused together but craning apart. May tries moving toward the light on one side, the side opposite where she came in; Cristofana leans in the other direction, but the pressure to settle into the other, to clip into oneness, is so intense that May can't breathe. At last she slumps—they do as one—breathless and gasping for air.

"What's the matter with you?" she howls back. "Your sister may be dead, but you *know* where you belong!"

Cristofana just howls harder, without words, as if to drown out the noise of May's voice in her head.

It hurts to speak. It hurts to hear.

"You made a home with them. . . . Even I can see that. . . . It's chaotic, like your brain . . . all odds and ends and feathers and broken toys, but it's home, Cristofana. They need you in it."

May feels her head shaking, though she isn't shaking it, feels her jaw clamp and her eyes tear up.

"I never asked to be needed. I have no wish—"

"It's not just about you!" May screams. "Don't you get that?" Breathing out, she feels the tension wane, their single body wearied for the moment beyond recall.

"I don't remember family," the other admits in a hoarse whisper. "What must I do?" She winces as if the question, or the imperative, hurts her head.

Everything hurts, thinks May, *throbs*, *aches* . . . Their body in revolt against itself.

May tries to imagine Marco asserting his role as a fourteenth-century man of the house. When church elders come knocking, requesting altarpieces and frescoes, and he has to worry again what the world thinks, about morals and ethics and social status and money, what will he do? How will he keep his nutso, thieving sex partner a secret or hide their hastily adopted child?

May tries to imagine Cristofana giving up her spells and wanderings to mend underwear and hold Pippa's restless hand in the pew on Sundays, and though there's something very wrong with this picture, what May wants to say, what she *would* say if she were more generous and less resentful of the brand her double has obviously left on the workshop, on Marco and Pippa: *You're already doing it.*

"Forgive them," she says instead, "and make them laugh. Quit stealing and waving that knife around. The sickness will pass, so think about the future now. He won't have you—won't keep you—if you can't behave."

"Behave?" Insolent and incredulous, Cristofana seems more herself again, which is reassuring, in a way. May feels the surge of resistance in her, the raw energy echoing all around in the dark air of the passage or whatever they're in, feels her own strength returning.

"At least in public. When it's over," May explains,

"and the world's normal again, he'll want his old family back, or what's left of it. He'll want to be proud of you . . . his new family."

"Is that love, Little Nun?" Cristofana scoffs, and as one, they spit into the dark of the portal. "That which tames us?"

"Yeah," she says. "I think it is, and what's wrong with that?"

There is a tearing pain, a violent jolt as Cristofana tries to rise and wrench free again.

May steels herself inside their single body, standing stern. "Just answer me! Why won't you let yourself love them?"

"I will tell you a story," threatens the voice in her head, her own voice, a stranger's. "A story about home." They settle together, sinking as one, kneeling and swaying like a drunk about to retch. "Once there was a little girl who lived in a little house in Firenze with her little family. So often and so fiercely did this girl beg to sail with her merchant father that he brought her back a magic tapestry, as blank as a summer sky.

"The fabric was fine like spider's silk, though her father swore it was made by a little worm that spun and spun. It came, he said, from the mysterious Far East, and should the girl hang this panel by her bed, it would give her leave to journey after him to faraway lands.

"It was a band of cloth the length and breadth of a door, as transparent as a window, with the shimmer of water. Anyplace she imagined on that surface, he said, she could visit by only stepping through. 'Do you see it, *uccellino?*' he would say, and the girl did. While he was away across the water, each night before bed, she traveled far and wide, visiting the menageries of exotic princes and sailing on wild seas where men speared great rubbery beasts the size of ships themselves, and she was patient and happy."

"Cristofana, this isn't exactly comfortable, you know. Could we have this conversation outside—?"

"Shhh," hisses the voice they share. "But then the girl's sister, her only confidant, went away forever to be a bride to Christ.

"Her father was gone for years at sea, and when her mother was murdered in the girl's own room, where the panel hung in place of her bed curtain, the blood splattered it.

"She lay beaten and broken for hours, this girl, or days, in a pain that sometimes blinded her, and the blood spoke to her.

"Her mother's ghost came and stood at the foot of the bed, flicking the fabric with long, lacquered nails.

'Child,' she said, 'it is just a curtain cut from an old bolt. Just a piece of dingy cloth. No more and no less. He fooled us both,' she complained, 'your father.'"

The voice fades out in a sigh, recovers, flows forceful again.

"When the midwife saved her and took her away to live, the little girl insisted on taking the panel with them.

"The first spell the witch taught her was to bleach away stains.

"Next they steeped the cloth in herbs and potions, boiling it with bone and feathers and ground mirror. They worked the cloth well and washed it, they wrung it and ironed it, and after, it was so fine and strong it never ripped, never wrinkled, only grew softer and stronger until it was 'like chain mail writ fine,' said the witch. And like a knight's armor it would be the girl's protection, for it would take her anywhere . . . and away from anywhere . . . as the time commanded.

'Are you sure this time?' the girl asked.

'I am sure of time,' said the witch, who was already ailing then, who had returned the ruby ring and taken to her bed. 'There is no thing surer.'

"Then she gestured to the cloth, pristine, as blank as her eyes would be within the hour. 'More study, child. More patience.'

"The girl was afraid to travel, afraid to be invisible, though with the witch gone, she had to learn—and learn well, for it kept her safe—but time passed, and she met a man, named Marco, who bade her rest in the safety of his gaze."

May stiffens.

"The body is a curious thing," the voice insists, "vulnerable to sickness, sores, and sloth, flea-bitten and foul, full of every indignity—piss, shit, blood, and ache—and mysterious humors that the physicians balance like accounts, and yet . . . and yet. The girl who had learned to be invisible would rather wear her form freely in the world, be an avid predator, never again prey, and she was never so happy to be alive in her body as when the artist painted her.

"When first he proposed his sittings, the girl squirmed and seethed and willed no man that right—to fix her in his sights and keep her still. She lacked patience with his veils and drapes, and the way he twisted her head on her neck and bade her look this way and bend that. Cramped and bored, she stood often, pacing in circles like a caged animal.

"But his patience worked its spell on her, and she came to trust him. Sometimes still, Marco hums for her"—May feels her head rise involuntarily, eyes seeking a face, a connection—"which none have done since

Mamma. Other times he sets Duck at her feet, like an anchor, and the infant clings on her legs, pleading a tune, whence the girl finds herself humming . . . like a mother.

"Thanks to Duck, the girl finds Mamma often in her thoughts now, though for years that ghost was banished.

"Thanks also to the little nun, who advised: *Forgive them.*

"The girl has forgiven everyone, it seems: Father, for becoming a merchant, for taking to sea for so very long and for leaving her and Mamma to bandits. Her sister, for vanishing into Christ's tent. She has forgiven Mamma her pride and folly, her love of jewels and ostentation, which drew envy as meat does dogs. She has forgiven the bandits who cut her mother's throat, beat and abused that mother's child, and left both for dead, who took all but the clothes on their backs and a ring their bloodlust blinded them to. She has forgiven Mamma for lying blue and swollen on the floor — too far away to reach as the doves from the eaves pecked her eyes — and the old midwife who came and chased the doves away, and wrapped the mother's body, and set the child's bones and fed her broth, and ultimately raised the orphan with love and taught her spells and gave her courage, but all for the price of a ruby ring.

She has forgiven the old witch for sawing away her mother's bloated finger before her eyes to secure that ring, and for first begging a child's permission to do so. She has forgiven the old woman, her savior, for requiring the ring and for dying on the eve of the Pest. She has forgiven her beloved Firenze for coming to resemble Hell. And she has forgiven God for sending a scourge beyond reckoning.

"Last but not least, she has forgiven her insufferable twin—and the artist they delight in in almost equal measure—for reminding her that forgiveness is as much a shade of love as ruby is a shade of red.

"The one soul she has not forgiven, the girl understood, that last time Marco studied her in profile with her gaze fixed on the ruby ring, is herself."

Feeling her strength returning, their strength, and the pressure to push back, May says, "This too shall pass," pushing against herself, her conjoined twin, with all her might, pushing, pushing, but not hard enough.

They tumble out onto the stony ground of the alley in a sprawl, Cristofana whole and solid, May in ghost form.

"The best one wins," her twin croons, brushing pebbles off her hands, grinning her devil's grin.

Feeling the strength drain out of her, feeling

despair rush into every cell her double has just vacated, May sighs, sinking to her spectral knees. "Here we go again."

"No, *bella.*" Cristofana laughs, lightly and truly. "You go. Only you. Did I not say? Your Li-um, though he tastes not of honey, is a most excellent scholar, and this night his searching scroll told me that the Pest leaves Florence soon. Any day now, we will be free again, and this city, Marco's bed, is not big enough for both of us. I was only waiting for you to show yourself."

"How do you know what he tastes like?" May snaps, gesturing wildly. "And what did you say about all . . . this?"

"To Li-um?" His name sounds obscene on her lips. "I told him nothing," she says with a shrug. "I let him have my body because he professed to need it so much. You starve your men, it seems, and I am left to fill what cups you leave empty."

"Do you know how lucky you are that I can't slap you right now?"

"My goal was to be you, was it not? It was what you would have done."

"Yeah?" May rages. "You think so?"

"I know it."

"You know shit."

"Then you must be a fool."

"I want what powers the portal," May says, changing the subject, "that panel or whatever it is, to take back with me."

"This is not possible."

"Then no deal. I want insurance that you won't come back."

"You have my word."

"Your word is worth exactly nothing."

"You amuse me, *bella*. I commend you, but now I must go. My family waits for me." She smiles her smug smile, her voice serious. "We are all we have."

Something wounded in her eyes makes May ache. Wouldn't it be funny, she thinks, if in some twisted way she ended up missing Cristofana, her drama and grandstanding, her stubborn strangeness?

It all happens very quickly—as a sequence of actions, it's almost anticlimactic—and in the instant before May backs through the portal, with their mirror eyes locked in mutual distrust, she feels an odd blend of grief and fondness. There's a hot flash of black, like a cosmic zipper closing, and when May juts out her hand, it smacks wall.

Liam is asleep on her bed, a deadweight over the covers, too exhausted even to feel May settle behind with a grateful sigh, spooning without touching him.

Hormones

"What's going on here?" It's barely light out yet, and Gwen's petite outline fills the doorway. May stiffens, remembering Liam — beside her, snoring in the bed.

Shit.

"And don't say *nothing*. He hasn't eaten in days, which is unheard of, and *you* . . . May, my God . . . I don't know what's up, but staying in bed for over a week and refusing a doctor isn't OK —"

"Gwen," Liam croaks under his breath, rolling toward her voice. "Things are kind of complicated with us right now."

"You're not pregnant . . . are you?"

"Ma, please. We really need you to stay out of this—"

Gwen cuts him off, her voice craning toward May, who hasn't had the nerve to turn and face her accuser yet. "May?"

May groans. "God . . . no." She rolls over as Liam sits upright, shaking the sleep out of his head. "This isn't what you think. It's—"

"Hormones," Li blurts helplessly, shielding his eyes as from too-bright sunlight. "Just hormones—"

If you only knew. May rolls back toward the wall with a sigh.

"Can we talk about this later?" Li adds in a small voice.

"Well, this *is* awkward. Do we need to get your parents involved, May?"

"No!" they both cry at once, and May rolls over again.

"Please, no," she says. "It'll all be fine now—I promise."

"I should have known this was going to happen," Gwen laments—and May is surprised to see traces of amusement on her guardian's face. "I guess I saw it coming."

Liam stands, rumpled, hiking his sagging jeans up. "Glad somebody did." He flashes an agonized look at May before escaping down the hall.

When Gwen can't get them in the same room together after that, when she can't *keep* them in a room together, she wants answers.

May doesn't have any. Liam apparently doesn't, either.

The day after his mom found them together, at dinner in the restaurant that evening, the first time their eyes met, May knew.

Cristofana wasn't kidding.

Something *had* happened. They hooked up—with Cristofana starring as May—and now he wants May to own up, acknowledge it. She can't, of course, so he's stopped looking at her that way. He's stopped looking at her at all.

He trains his eyes away, pulls out his cell again, and starts pretending to e-mail his friends, and May lets him.

Would Li believe her if she told him—tried to tell him—the truth? They'd joked about him running into Cristofana, and it was a good joke, but it wasn't this, and this wasn't funny. She could *try* to explain, but how could he believe it was anything but her lame attempt to elude "emotional responsibility," as her mom or Gwen might say?

Um, yeah . . . that wasn't me. It was my double. Good one.

For spite, May daydreams of going back to be with Marco again. She'll tell him everything . . . about Cristofana, Li, her parents . . . and the beautiful artist won't understand a word she's saying. He'll just look at her with those sorrowful, knowing eyes, and put his hands on her again, and it will be fine. He'll tell her all about the plague and what it did to him, his family, his world, and she won't understand, either, and they'll kiss until their lips are chapped and bruised, and it will be all right.

May wants to feel safe again the way she did when she woke up wrapped in that old blanket, and he was there calmly eating his apple, watching her for just that one night as he had the day they met, that first time in the workshop, before Cristofana stepped into their story and confused everything.

In her defense, May did try to explain one evening, over their dinner of bread and cheese and olives, watching Pippa prance in babbling circles, covered in crumbs. May floated the words she had tried hard to memorize in the future like so many balloons—*altro, gemello, attento*—but if Marco understood, he didn't show it, only cleared their wooden plates and led her by the hand to a far wall where canvases were propped. It was the first time he voluntarily shared his work with her, and as he flipped through, pausing at first one and then another, May's eyes filled with tears.

Perhaps he *did* know the difference—only she and Cristofana were both phantoms to him, figments of his imagination. If his paintings were any indication, that mental landscape was haunted by every possible demon.

May has tried since not to think about the paintings he showed her, figures frightening and beautiful, of Cristofana nude and stunning, imbued with unimaginable dignity and grace. Had he *disguised* her? Was that what art did? Or was Cristofana someone else for him completely?

Who had she been for Liam?

May understands that she was lucky to get out of Old Florence alive, to get home again. But Cristofana was just as lucky.

In her quest to avoid Liam and the conversation they aren't having about the sex they didn't have (not as far as she's concerned), May has decided to visit every single art museum and Medici gallery in Florence.

Each morning she kisses Gwen on the back of the head — a slave to her own distraction, Gwen has forgiven them, it seems, and almost never lifts her eyes from her morning newspaper — slips out of the quiet apartment, orders a cappuccino, and sits on the curb, circling a new destination on her guidebook map while pigeons crowd around and peck her backpack.

By the time May determines her day's route, her coffee is cold and as bitter as bark, but it's all part of the ritual. The goal is to be outdoors before it gets too hot — and before Liam gets up.

They've managed to avoid each other completely for three days, with one or the other begging out sick at dinner.

Their one and only conversation about the hookup was a disaster, all blush and stammer and things unsaid. Whatever Cristofana did to him or let him do to her wasn't for May to know.

Liam took one look at her and knew things weren't right. "We could go out for a beer again," he tried. "Or hike up to Fiesole."

Silence.

"So it was a mistake."

It wasn't really a question, and he looked away as soon as he said it, already resigned, because her eyes must have agreed. Though May wasn't sure what she was agreeing with or to.

"And you regret it."

Silence.

Regret what? A sure way to ruin their friendship?

"I get that. I do. But you were pretty enthusiastic at the time—"

May almost snarled then because the words backed up in her throat. She couldn't speak, couldn't stand to think about Cristofana touching him the way she, May, had touched Marco. *That* way. With all that. *And she* would, *too*, May thought—with a hypocrite's fury. *Just to spite me.*

May didn't blame Liam, but she did. For being weak enough to fall for it. For not seeing through her selfish double. For not *seeing*. Not believing his own eyes, and ears, and hands.

How lonely May feels, wandering through palaces and cathedrals every day—and how weirdly, exasperatingly hopeful. Today she's settled on the Chapel of the Magi in Palazzo Medici Riccardi.

At first the building seems little more than a

government office, but when she actually finds her way inside to the chapel, it's breathtaking. For a good fifteen minutes, May sits half lotus on the floor.

Every inch of the space not given over to intricate mosaics or gilt gold or wooden stalls seems to be frescoed over. The paintings depict a procession of humans and animals winding among white rocks and slender tree trunks. The colors are delicate and dizzying, and in the sky, clouds and birds are hard to separate. Everything, from the castle in the background to the neat olive-tree-lined hills to the elaborate fabric patterns, soft grass, and wavy pageboy hair, tempts you to touch it. A jaguar sits by a man on horseback while a hawk eats its lunch, and everyone seems serene but also purposeful. In a little niche against the back wall is an altarpiece painted on wood; here, set a little apart, is what everyone's traveling to, the stable of the Holy Family.

Every now and then on outings like this one, spotting an idle docent or bored-looking security guard, May fishes a rumpled sticky note from her jeans pocket and reveals the name copied there, the one she committed to memory, from letters and shipping documents in the workshop. "Have you ever heard of this painter?" *Marco Veronese*.

It would be easy enough to get Gwen's advice on how to track down an artist who isn't online—if there's a more direct way, Gwen would happily share it at length — but May wants this research for herself. It's private.

"When was he working?" they ask.

"Before the Renaissance," May explains. "During the plague in Florence."

"A minor artist, probably. What were his subjects?"

Thinking back to the first sketch she saw on his easel, of the gargoyle looming out over a doomed city, May tries to reply. "He did a lot of portraits and nudes," she'd say, "and scary things, smiling skeletons and demons, screaming women, gargoyles, stuff like that."

The docent or security guard would smile indulgently. "Back then and into the Renaissance, painters did mainly commissions for the Church. Private portraits were rare, nudes especially, given the influence of Church authorities. There were many masters in those decades. Too many to name."

And? Her face must have asked.

"That name, Marco Veronese, means nothing to me, I'm afraid. Paolo Veronese, yes. Marco, no."

All her museum hopping has a happy side effect in that it makes Gwen insanely happy. May has even finished two of the three essays due when school starts in a week.

Senior year . . . in Vermont.

And she's made her decision, though it wasn't easy. She'll miss her mom — so much — but it didn't make sense to uproot her whole life now, when college would just uproot it all over again.

Emerging from the shower the next morning, full of that restlessness you feel near the end of a trip, with your mind tugging toward the future, May fishes her charger out of her jam-packed suitcase, plugs in the phone, and watches the screen light up. While her battery recharges, May pats her long hair dry with a towel, dips her head, and winds it all up into a turban.

She still feels edgy at times, as if Cristofana might show up at any moment and press-gang her into the vicious past again, but May's learning to live with not knowing. Maybe because deep down, she no longer believes it will happen.

Imagining Liam asleep on the other side of the wall, she thinks, *That's it*, glancing around at the now-bare room, saying good-bye in mind to that strange little family to which she did and didn't belong, accepting at last that they are a family, and that she's too young to contemplate their reality or belong in it. May has a family of her own, and if Cristofana and the others have taught her anything, it's that no family is perfect.

We are all we have.

May fetches her phone and scrolls through her texts and voice mails.

Are you my mother?

May longs for her like a child.

Are you really?

Right now she wants nothing more than to be a little girl again. She opens her Contacts screen. After scrolling impatiently, she highlights MOM, and her mom answers on the first ring.

Before and After

That night, their last in Florence, neither she nor Liam is willing to sit dinner out. It's a beautiful night on the cusp of September. The streets are full of laughter and distant music and the smells of garlic and coffee. The city is lit like a fairy tale.

May feels light, almost ebullient, after her conversation with her mom. She cried, hearing her voice for the first time all summer. Her mom cried harder. After, they laughed that snorting, sobbing laughter that's borderline hysterical, saying over and over how sorry they were.

Gwen does all the talking while they wait for their meal but lets things settle into an almost comfortable silence over dessert. They share one last trough of tiramisu, licking their spoons thoughtfully, and then, out of the blue, Gwen says she has to go meet a friend. "Last night here and all. I've already paid the bill," she says. "I trust you two can get back to the apartment in one piece?"

May smiles sheepishly, looking away when her gaze meets Liam's. "I think that can be arranged."

"OK, then." Laying her napkin on the tablecloth, Gwen walks around and kisses the tops of their two heads, breezing out without so much as a backward glance.

The silence gets oppressive fast, so May murmurs, "I talked to both my parents today."

"Yeah?" He's visibly relieved. "Gwen thought maybe you did. I'm glad to hear it."

"It was weird," she admits, "how really normal they sound. Different but normal."

For a while he doesn't say anything; then he looks right into her eyes, and she fights not to look away. "I'm sort of hoping we'll get to that place, too."

"Different?"

"But normal."

Suddenly all the good she felt, all the relief, leaks

away, leaving her with an angry buzzing in her blood. *Everything that's yours. . . .*

"How can you ask me to do that? Act normal? I can't." She stands abruptly, her napkin slipping to the floor, and winds her way around tables and past the hostess stand with her heart hammering.

She weaves through the crowd mobbing the front door and can't explain why she starts running when she hits the curb, when she senses him catching up, except that Liam isn't hers and she isn't his, and there is no such thing; people don't own other people or belong to them, and even if it means she has to be an idiot tripping over the cobblestones, she doesn't have to hear it; she doesn't have to pretend otherwise.

He's stopped saying her name. He doesn't seem to want to calm her down anymore or even catch up to her. He just walks behind at a fast clip, and when it finally sinks in that he isn't going to give up and let her walk home alone in the dark, she stops and reels to face him. In the same moment, she realizes where they are, in that narrow alley near the Misericordia, leading away from Piazza del Duomo—Via della Morte, Way of Death.

To her left is the plaque explaining how a daughter of the noble house of Amieri got sick during a bout of plague. She looked dead, so they shut her up in her husband's ancestral vault in a cemetery between the cathedral and campanile. Ginevra woke in a panic, squirmed out of her shroud, raised the stone slab, and fled in terror from the vault, returning wraithlike to her husband's home. When he and her father both refused her, Ginevra braved the home of her forbidden love, young Rondinelli, and was received. Her marriage to Agolanti was annulled, and she was able to marry her true love.

May is still trying to catch her breath, but as she and Liam stand there wondering what to do or say, she imagines that poor woman waking up in her pitch-black tomb, alive but utterly transformed, severed from her past and all she took for granted, her life divided by the plague into before and after. But at that fateful moment of waking, she was just there, poised in the present, between no more and not yet.

Slowly and gently, Li walks her backward to the wall, enclosing her there with an arm on either side, laying his palms flat on the stone, and she feels like some kind of wild animal he's calming. They catch their collective breath, and May doesn't try to get away or shove him back. She wants the warmth of him, the comfort in what's familiar; she's curious, too, about what's not.

Normal but different.

"Did you even tell them how you felt before you left?" he demands. "I've been meaning to ask. Did you tell them you were pissed? That you had an opinion?"

"I go quietly," she complains, looking away. "That's what I do. What difference would it make?"

"Absolutely none, but it might've felt good."

"No. I didn't tell them, and I'm not telling you, either."

He tries to cup her chin, and she jerks her face aside, feeling the closeness of his body, his ready warmth.

"Yeah, you piss me off," she relents. "They piss me off. Everyone pisses me off."

"Well, congratulations, May, and welcome to the real world. People get mad here and make mistakes and shit on each other and are even wrong sometimes."

Now she does try to shove him, aware that to people passing at the mouth of the alley they must look like a crime scene in the making. He doesn't budge, so she shoves him again. "Fuck you."

"I'm all for it," he says wryly, almost apologetically, under his breath.

She kicks him in the shin, not hard, but hard enough to take him off guard. He turns with a guilty smirk, back against the wall for balance, and gradually slides onto his rear, at which point she kicks him in the thigh, halfheartedly . . . a little kid winding down in a tantrum. He grabs her ankle and urges her down with his hands until she kneels in front of him, and for a second they jostle and bump heads until finally she lets him fold her in his arms, into his worn-soft T-shirt and his smell. "It wasn't me," she sobs, sloppy and ecstatic and relieved. *How could you do that?* . . . "It wasn't—"

"Look," he says, his voice low in her ear, "it was, for me." He leans close and kisses her lightly, tipping up her chin to make her look at him. "I don't know what you're talking about half the time, but who the hell else would it be?"

WHAT I DID ON MY SUMMER VACATION

"Are you ready for this?" May asks, rolling to face him.

Their first flight's delayed, the gate waiting room is all but deserted, and she and Liam lie afloat on a sea of carpet, heads propped on suitcases, surrounded by a fairy ring of drink cups and snack wrappers, cells, iPods, and essay fragments.

Across the aisle, Gwen hunches on her plastic chair, scribbling on a yellow legal pad and swilling espresso.

"Home, you mean?"

The sight of him sawing at an apple with a plastic knife suddenly rivets May; for half a second his concentration in profile reminds her of Marco, of that rush moment when she woke wrapped in his blanket with his liquid eyes intent on her over the green of apple.

"Life?" Liam asks, answering his own question. "Yeah, ready as I'll ever be. What about you?"

May shrugs, thinking about the postcard in her backpack and of some myth or tradition Gwen related once about souls traveling in packs from life to life, through birth and death and rebirth, recycling and magnetically reengaging every chance they got.

She lets Liam stuff a jagged wedge of apple into her mouth and wonders irrationally — the thought making her giddy, almost sick — if maybe Liam was once Marco. She keeps thinking of them in tandem. Would that make *her* Cristofana? *We share the same soul.* She has to smile at the thought, chewing, and Liam gives up on the rest of the already browning apple. He rolls sideways, curious, propped on his elbow to look at her.

They speak at almost the same time:

"Do you believe in past lives?" she asks.

"What'd you buy in the museum shop?" he asks.

"Not really," he says.

"Just a postcard," she says.

"Not even a little?" she asks.

"Can I see?" he asks.

"No."

"No." It's playful, her refusal, but she means it.

On the one hand, showing Liam the postcard would explain a lot. It might even help him believe her. He's never said outright that he didn't, but Liam is a guy who likes math, formulas, certainty. He must figure that if he can make sense of physics, he can make sense of anything, but Cristofana inhabits a universe all her own, one stitched together with blood spells and lies and nursery rhymes. It's no world for Liam. It's no world for May, either, and maybe in the end, forgetting will be easier (for both of them) than just not getting it.

The postcard could be a kind of proof. But for some reason, May doesn't want to explain it, doesn't want it justified, dissected, categorized, or cured. She wants to keep it for herself. *What I did on my summer vacation . . .*

According to the caption, the painting on the postcard (*Untitled; Italy, circa 1350; artist unknown*) was "an unusual/anachronistic early example of surrealist technique."

On the postcard is the portrait of a young woman with long dirty-blond hair beside an ornately carved floor-length mirror with a little girl clinging to her leg. The woman's expression is playful, withholding with a hint of wickedness. But her reflection in the mirror—

identical, apart from a dress that seems a plainer shadow of its counterpart—wears a completely different expression. The features are the same, but the reflection's face is grave and secretive, thoughtful, almost startled. The fact that the two don't match makes the picture disturbing to look at. And fascinating.

To avoid Liam's puzzled eyes, May starts organizing and flipping through scattered essay pages. Remembering the history lesson that Liam inadvertently gave Cristofana, May finds confirmation in the paper she started on bioterrorism and the path of the plague. *The Black Death ended in September 1348,* she reads, smiling to herself. The painting in the postcard is dated 1350. Safe bet, then, that Marco, Cristofana, and Pippa all survived the end days of the plague . . . and managed to stick together. At least for a couple of years.

Maybe Cristofana managed to change, after all.

Maybe Marco tamed her.

Looking up, May notes Gwen asleep in her hard airport chair, her back straight and the straps of her handbag wound severely around her right hand. Sliding their trash aside, May pivots, shifting her weight to lay her head on Liam's chest. She hopes he'll reach around and stroke her face, and he does, looking down at her with eyes the same relentless blue as the sky in the wall of windows behind them. "You gonna miss Chicago at Princeton?" she asks, staring hard at him, memorizing him.

"Not like I'll miss you."

There it is, plain and simple, and now he's waiting for an answer, for a sign.

"But Jersey's closer to Boston," he says, "than Second City."

"I don't know what school I'll get into," she protests, looking away. She's actually kind of crazily thinking premed. "There's so much. . . . I'm not sure I want to be with anyone now. Not sure I *can* be. But if I could"—he doesn't seem to need May to say more, but she does, aware of his heat and his heartbeat beneath her—"it would be you."

"Yeah. Me too," Liam says, tilting his head in that rakish way of his. "Both of you."

May mock pounds on him, and they roll and tussle. She pins him under, straddling him until a buttoned-up businessman formerly concealed in a seat behind a pillar—the only other human (now) in sight besides the snoring Gwen—leans to the side and clears his throat meaningfully as if to say, *Get a hotel room*, and May scrabbles like a crab out of view behind the pillar, Liam moving with her. They huddle back there like children, laughing mutely and hysterically, and May will never feel so extraordinarily normal again.